THE HERO AND THE HELLION

A STEAMY REGENCY HISTORICAL ROMANCE

AVA DEVLIN

The Hero and the Hellion

The Somerton Scandals - Book 3

Ava Devlin

Copyright © 2020 by Ava Devlin

All rights reserved. This book or any portion thereof
may not be reproduced or used in any manner whatsoever
without the express written permission of the publisher
except for the use of brief quotations in a book review.

Printed in the United States of America

First Printing, 2020

http://avadevlin.com

Contact the author at ava@avadevlin.com

Cover art by BZN Studio Designs

http://covers.bzndesignstudios.com

Copyediting by Claudette Cruz

https://www.theeditingsweetheart.com/

❦ Created with Vellum

FREE EBOOK

Discover the scandal that started them all! The sweet and steamy prequel novella The Dreamer and the Debutante *reveals the secrets that kicked off the Somerton Scandals and the history between Callum and Heloise.*

Get your FREE copy now at http://avadevlin.com

PROLOGUE

The Princess and the Stable Boy
A Fairy Tale by Heloise Somers for Caroline Cunningham

There once was a Princess who wished to be a commoner and a Stable Boy who wished to be a knight. The Princess dreamed of a life in the village, picking flowers and milking cows, free to explore the wilderness and marry for love. The Stable Boy imagined a life of pleasure and wealth, where he would perform acts of great heroism and never have to bow and scrape to those that were born as his betters.

Despite their differences, the Princess and the Stable Boy played together as children. They didn't know, until many years had passed by, that the two were destined for very different worlds, and that their friendship must someday end. They got into mischief together and had wonderful fun, until one day, the Stable Boy was injured during one of their games and had to wear his arm in a sling.

The Princess's brother, the King, was furious with her and told her she would be sent away to learn how to be a proper lady. She cried and cried, feeling terribly guilty for how she'd hurt her beloved friend, and fearing what life might be like away from the palace.

On the day she was to be sent off, the Princess sneaked into the stables to say goodbye to her best friend and to apologize to him for how he was hurt. The Stable Boy smiled and showed off his sling, insisting that he was proud to finally have a battle scar that befitted a knight. The Princess was overcome with love for her friend and kissed him right on the lips! To her great surprise, he kissed her right back, holding her close with his one unbroken arm.

In that moment, the Princess knew that the Stable Boy would be her one true love.

Years passed by, and the Princess did indeed learn how to be a lady. Without her best friend in attendance, she often got caught playing her pranks and had no one to laugh with about her mischief. Still, she learned what was expected of her, and did her best to hide her spirit beneath a mask of what was proper.

When the Princess finally returned to her kingdom, there was a great storm. The night sky lit up with bolts of lightning and terrible booms of thunder as the carriage rocked and swayed its way to the castle. When she finally arrived and the door to the carriage opened, the first person the Princess saw was her old friend, the Stable Boy, who had grown into a strapping and very handsome man.

Prologue

Though she was expected to take her place at her brother's side as a respectable young woman, the Princess sneaked out time and again to see her old friend, the Stable Boy. Both of them remembered that long-ago kiss, and neither could resist the temptation to kiss again, all these years later. In this way, the two fell in love, keeping their forbidden romance a secret from the King and all his servants.

The Stable Boy took the Princess riding across magical mountains, discovering enchanted caves and beautiful wildflowers. They made plans to someday become exactly who they'd always wished, and marry to live happily ever after. They were very much in love.

But becoming a knight was no easy feat, and the Stable Boy had to go into battle to earn his new status and prove his worth. He became a hero, writing to his fellow servants at the castle about his feats of glory, all while the Princess kept an open ear, hoping to hear how he fared.

Meanwhile, the Princess discovered that she was to have a child, a magical little girl, who would be at once both a commoner and a royal, and enjoy the best of both of those worlds. The new Little Princess was born at the end of springtime, with all of the roses and bluebells and daisies and daffodils bursting into vibrant bloom to herald the summer. She became very beloved by the King and his people, and now that she was a mother, the Princess could remain at the castle to care for her little girl.

In this way, both the Princess and the Stable Boy got what they once had wished for, though neither could have predicted how their stories would unfold. The Princess became a commoner, living amongst the townspeople with her basket of wildflowers, and the Stable Boy became a knight, decorated for his bravery in battle.

The Little Princess grew up in a world where she would be able to choose which path she wished to take, and her future was still ahead of her, waiting for the day she grew up.

1

*I*t was snowing again.

Heloise Somers stared out the window of her bedroom, watching the lazy drift of snowflakes whirl and spin against the bright shafts of moonlight. The onset of winter this year had been a sudden thing. One day it was a chilly, but colorful autumn in golden light, and then, as though they had slept for a year rather than just a night, the people of Somerton awoke to find a blanket of white on the ground. For the last month, the snows had come almost daily, drowning the spectacular landscape of Yorkshire in an even, white layer of frost, like a gown of satin and lace, sewn for the moors.

There was no telling what hour it was. This was the third time in a week that she'd found herself ripped from a restful slumber, twisted in her sheets in a cold sweat, battling the demons of her mind, until she rose, panting and gasping for air, haunted by the intensity of her dreams.

Were they nightmares? Could something that began as

utter, blissful perfection count as a nightmare? Sometimes she awoke before the narrative in her fantasy world turned dark, before the clouds began to gather over the story that was only half told. It didn't matter. Wherever in the plot she managed to escape to the waking world, she still found herself wrapped in a heavy cloak of sadness.

She sighed, frustrated with herself, and flicked at the curtains in irritation.

In her dreams, the view from this window would have been much greener, wild and lush under a blistering summer sun. In her dreams, the clouds gathered in great, heavy sacks of gray and silver and unleashed a torrent of whipping, shining rain upon the earth. The wind sent up glorious wildflowers and thickets of tall grass. She could see herself, years younger, clinging to the back of her bay mare as they galloped across the green with joyous abandon.

Surely anyone who dreamt of such a beautiful, warm summer would feel despondent upon waking to remember that the dead of winter was upon them! Surely it was only that. She preferred long days and warm breezes, after all. Who didn't?

It wasn't the other thing.

Dreaming of him was only happy and blissful in the distorted reality of dreams, where the truth of the years since dissolved into a strange, forgotten suspension, drowned out by the whims of silly sentimentality. They painted scenarios that ruined a good night's sleep with their idiotic idealism.

She shook her head, clicking her tongue with impatience, and turned her back on the stark landscape without. She

Chapter 1

snatched her dressing gown from its post and wrapped it around her body, cinching it just slightly tighter than necessary at the waist. Perhaps a bit of discomfort would pull her completely back to reality before she attempted to sleep again.

She was a different person now than she'd been that summer. The wild Heloise who'd played tricks and fallen in love was gone, and good riddance. She had been young and naive, reckless with her body and heart, and it didn't matter anymore anyway. It was long past.

This torment was the fault of that damned book. It had been at least a year since she'd dreamt of Callum Laughlin, but ever since she was given that godforsaken book, he seemed to haunt her every time the moon rose! She had a mind to dig it out of the trunk at the foot of her bed and toss it out the window. It would be buried in snow, and come spring, only a rotting mush of papers would remain, with no spiky handwriting professing a long-forgotten love. Perhaps that would break the spell it had cast upon her.

No, she corrected herself, it was surely a curse or a hex. Simple spellcraft would never conjure something so painful.

Like all such dark magic, the book was nothing special in and of itself, just a penny book from a shop in France with a salaciously embellished retelling of the romance between Caesar and Cleopatra. The story had meant something to the two of them, once, but that was beside the point. It was the inscription inside that had sent her world asunder, delivered some 4 years after its arrival at the wrong address in Bath-Spa, where it had languished to her ignorance while her resentment had grown.

Then, at the most unexpected moment, she'd been handed the cursed thing and had seen the spiky handwriting inside.

Thinking of you Always ...

Forever Yours - C.L.

It would have been better to never have known he had sent it, all those years ago. It would have been preferable to carry on, believing he'd left her behind completely. Now, she had to bear the burden of knowing that he had not forgotten her, nor had he intended to leave her for good. Now, she had to wonder what had happened in the years since he'd gone to war and if he thought of her still. Ignorance truly was bliss.

She didn't bother with slippers, flinging her door open to escape into the heart of the house. Something about her bare feet pacing carefully across the floor at the witching hour felt more honest to her, more primal. The dower house was not as large nor as grand as the manor house on the hill, though her mother had outfitted it beautifully upon taking up her station here as dowager viscountess.

Heloise never thought she'd consider anywhere but her childhood bedroom a true home, but it had been a kind of relief to come here. She was able to have both the surroundings of Somerton as a familiar comfort and a blank slate, all at once.

Without warm embers from a fireplace nor hot coals in a bed warmer, tucked snugly beneath the blankets, the halls bit into the skin with their chill. It was a welcome sort of discomfort, a reminder to live within the waking world rather than that of dreams. She shivered, crossing her arms over her body, and quickened her pace just a bit. All that mattered was right now, here in Somerton, some months after her daughter turned three years of age.

The door to the nursery was well oiled and silent as she pushed it open, waiting a moment for her eyes to adjust to the darkness within. Caroline had finally outgrown her crib this winter, and lay curled on a tiny child's bed, slick with wood polish that managed to gleam, even in the dark. She had her thumb in her mouth and her rag doll clutched to her side. Her mess of auburn hair was spread around her in a halo as she floated from dream to dream. Nothing had ever been so precious in all the world.

This was why she couldn't throw the book away.

Some day, her daughter would ask about her father, and this would be the one token of his love that she could pass along. One day, when Callie was old enough to really understand the truth of her birth, she deserved this little piece of that torrential summer that had produced her. It was young love, for certain, and perhaps more irrational than anything else, but it *had* been love that created her darling girl. Heloise wanted her to know that, to feel that she was the product of something pure and joyous and without regret.

She leaned her head against the doorframe, her chest clenching with emotion as the dreamy utopia she'd imagined in her sleep began to dissipate into the stark reality of the night. If Callum ever returned from the war, perhaps he would have a chance to know his daughter. Would it be a gift or a curse to tell him he'd sired a child? Surely he deserved to move on with his life, as she had, unburdened by the impulsive choices they'd made that summer. If he survived the danger he'd put himself in, she would have to think long and hard about whether or not to reveal this thing to him.

Perhaps it should be Callie's choice, when she was old enough to understand.

She wanted to go sit on the edge of the little bed and stroke her daughter's hair. Nothing would bring her back from the reverie of her haunted dreams like touching her child. The only thing that held her back from doing just that was knowing that it would cause the girl to stir and wake, which was not fair after she'd finally adjusted to this new bed.

It had been quite an effort moving her into a proper bed this autumn. They had found her on more than one occasion attempting to climb back into the old crib.

Change was hard. No one knew that as well as Heloise Somers.

She bit her lip against the urge to shiver as the cold from the halls settled into her bones. She slipped out of the nursery and secured the door, not wishing to allow the cold into the room where Callie slept.

Her hair was braided, falling nearly to her waist, and leaving the slender column of her neck exposed to the cool night air. She had half a mind to unbraid it and simply sleep with a warm cloak of vibrant red around her, perhaps protecting her from the mystical whims of the winter.

If her old classmate, the superstitious Miss Tatiana Everstead, were still in the manor, she might go to her for some eclectic cure to her dreams. It had been surreal having so many of the girls from finishing school flitting around the grounds all autumn, each of them a strange contradiction of

Chapter 1

newfound maturity and enduring personality. If Tia had consulted her deck of tarot cards some months ago and revealed to Heloise that her childhood nemesis, Miss Gloriana Blakely, would soon be marrying into the Somers family, she would have recoiled in abject horror.

It was strange, wasn't it? Time unfolded in the most unexpected ways, changing people before they even realized anything was amiss. On the night Heloise had realized her brother Alex was in love with a girl she'd once professed to hate, it had somehow filled her heart with warmth instead of ice. She chuckled quietly to herself as she made her way back to her bedroom, remembering the astounded reaction of her brothers when they'd come upon Heloise and Gloriana, heads together, as they planned the particulars of the upcoming wedding.

It was simply more proof that the girl she'd been four years ago was well and truly put to rest, and a steadier, more responsible Heloise Somers had emerged in her place. It wasn't that she was suddenly enamored of Gloriana. She simply realized that being helpful and supportive was the thing that would best serve her family, and she'd come to understand that family was all that truly mattered in this life. If becoming pregnant out of wedlock had taught her anything, it was that her family loved her, each in their own slightly infuriating way.

She closed herself quietly back into her bedroom and hurried across the floor to find her place back beneath the warmth of her blankets, dressing gown and all, her braid coiled around her like a tether.

Perhaps, she reflected, she should tell herself a story to soothe her back to sleep. It worked very well with both her daughter and her nephew when they were restless. She had found she was rather good at making up stories and imparting little lessons within them. Callie's favorite, however, was likely the last thing Heloise needed to reflect upon right now.

After all, she was no princess, and Callum Laughlin, wherever he was, was no longer a stable boy.

2

Callum Laughlin loved the full moon.

Even on a night like this one, where the frigid waters lapping up against the coast sent a spritz of ice onto anyone who dared tread too close, that brilliant blue light would lift his spirits.

His return to England had been, thus far, quite the opposite of the mythic "warm" welcome. The Thames was frozen solid, and therefore he'd had to dock a ways from the city, where booking a stage that went so far north as Yorkshire might as well have been a Herculean quest. Still, he was determined to conquer this latest challenge and ideally reach Somerton before the New Year.

"Which trunk is yours, sir?" a porter shouted, his collar pulled up so far that Callum could scarcely make out the man's face.

"No trunk," he replied over the whistling of the wind. "Just this pack!"

The porter squinted at him, but waved him off the docking area rather than comment, where it was only a short walk up to a little hamlet that sat on the water. He imagined his choices for the evening were either a last-call stage into London or a night in the emptiest inn.

For the first time, he could afford whichever he liked. If it weren't so damned cold and if he weren't so damned eager to get home, he might have relished the concept of returning to British shores and indulging in a bit of fanciful leisure. After all, he had spent his formative years gazing pie-eyed at his betters and wondering what it must be like to be a man of means.

The other soldiers from the ship had already split off toward a lively-looking tavern that spilled bright light into the thoroughfare. Even from the port, Callum had been able to make out the strains of raucous music, welcoming in a contingent of young men who were starved for luxury and warmth.

He chuckled, shaking his head as he adjusted the meager belongings on his back. Perhaps the true irony of coming into means of his own lay in losing the desire to truly indulge in them. Even with a battalion of brothers-in-arms about, with no call to duty hovering on the horizon which might interrupt a lively night of cards and ale, all he wanted to do was locate a stagecoach and get underway toward Somerton.

He hadn't told his mother that he was coming. Brenda Laughlin was always such fun when surprised, after all. He wagered after she'd boxed his ears for startling her so, she'd turn to biscuits and sweets and a freshly turned-down bed, all the while fussing and sighing and

Chapter 2

demanding he tell her everything he'd experienced abroad.

A lot of the boys in his regiment had waxed poetic about the day they might return to their own beds, but Callum wagered his carefully curated loft above the stable stalls had long been repurposed. It would be enough to simply be back on the grounds, even if it was too cold to smell the hay and lavish relish the breeze.

Home was much more than a bed, he supposed, even if his little loft had been particularly good. The whole reason he'd gone to war was to rise above living with horses, wasn't it? He knew that, rationally. It was only that a few days to return to everything familiar and safe that had preceded his rapid tumble into manhood would have been a lovely prospect, for a short time.

He breathed out a foggy breath into the night air, stomping the wet sand from his boots at the threshold of a tiny boarding house with a crooked sign out front. The inside, perhaps as a merit of its size, was blissfully warm and cozy, and the instant he entered, a young barmaid with bright red hair shot up from her place at the hearth to assist him.

His heart lodged somewhere between his sternum and his throat at the sight of her, rushing over with an enthusiastic smile on her freckled face. She didn't look like Heloise, not really. Up close, she was too buxom, her nose too flat, her eyes a murky brown rather than sparkling green. Still, he found himself rooted to the spot, barely able to breathe as she approached him, chattering away.

He could scarcely account for acknowledging her before he found himself plopped into a chair next to the fire, a warm bowl of soup in front of him, and a flagon of cider in his hand.

The barmaid had taken notice of his reaction to her, and blushed prettily when she drew near. "The stage won't be back until morning, sir. We've beds available though, if you've a need. We'll have you set off to London first thing tomorrow."

He nodded, patting at his jacket to find his coin purse, but the barmaid stopped him with a gentle hand to his arm. "You can settle up with Pa in the morning. If you find the loft lacking in warmth, do let us know," she said as she bit her lip, lashes fluttering, "we'll make sure you're comfortable."

Callum gave what he hoped was a polite smile and nodded to the young woman, making a show of reaching for his spoon as though he were a man scarcely fed for a long time. She hovered near the table, anxiously watching him take bite after bite. Finally, after a few moments of patient waiting, the maid gave a disappointed sigh and sulked off back to her duties.

Perhaps it would be a relief, he thought, to sleep the night through, to change into dry clothes at the very least, before setting off. Once in London, he could easily find transportation north, though it'd be slow going with the cold. If he was lucky, he'd arrive with plenty of time to ring in the new year at Somerton, an occasion full of hope for the days yet to come.

It had been four years since he'd set eyes on Heloise Somers, and somehow even now, starved for human contact and frozen to the bone, a pretty girl with blazing red hair clearly hoping for a spot in his bed was too dim a candle in her shadow to tempt him. He had wanted no other woman in the wake she left behind. He hid a smile in his spoon as he remembered that morning, after they'd been intimate the first time, to find the only blood on the sheets was his own and his arms raked with scratches from her passion.

Though she had been the maiden and he the experienced lover, in the aftermath of their frenzied coupling, he had felt like a damsel in a tower who'd been ravished by a lusty lord. Despite knowing he should feel some wound to his masculinity, it had only inflamed him more. There was never going to be another girl like Heloise, no matter how hard he looked.

He could only hope that she would be pleased to see him. He could pray that she hadn't pledged herself to another in his absence. He had to believe that she was still his to claim. It was the only thing that had kept him going through the smoke and racket of the war. It had been the sole comfort as he'd trudged into misery after misery, battle after battle, in a world where home felt like a long-abandoned dream.

"Away on leave or here to stay?" a man with a round belly and a bald head inquired, coming to retrieve his empty bowl.

"Here to stay," Callum replied, startled to realize he'd eaten everything set in front of him. He quaffed the remainder of his cider and handed the glass to the man as well. "It's strange to be back home, to be honest."

The man nodded, sizing Callum up where he sat. "Might I ask your name?"

"Laughlin," Callum said, noting the strength of the man's

build and his apparent interest in a returned soldier. "Lieutenant," he added, knowing the question of his rank went unspoken between them. "Four years away."

"Light packer, eh, Lieutenant?" the man replied with a raise of his eyebrows and a nod to the pack of belongings Callum had tossed under his chair. "Back when I served, any officer would have at least three times the luggage."

"Well, that was the trick," Callum said with a laugh, "they gave me the title and then kicked me out before it could go to my head."

The man had given him a curious look, but Callum wasn't looking for company, neither from a fellow ex-soldier nor his eager daughter. There were years ahead if he wanted to reminisce about the war, perhaps when it was farther behind him. All he wanted right now was the quickest avenue back home.

With a belly full of warmth, a fire crackling just below, and at long last, a bed that didn't swing with the current, Callum Laughlin found his eyelids heavy and his thoughts winding toward dreams the instant he pulled the covers up around his neck.

Soon, he'd see them all again: his mother and Heloise and his cat, Nero. Even stuffy Lord Somers would be a welcome sight. He remembered with a sleepy half smile that now there was also a *Lady* Somers by his side. That would be most curious indeed.

All he wanted in the world was to be home, and for Heloise Somers to find him once again, under the light of the full moon.

3

"Well!" gasped Abigail Collins, shooting to her feet. "Aren't you properly turned out! Is today the day?"

"Sit down, Abby!" Heloise tutted, smiling despite the rebuke as the heavily pregnant woman waddled forward to help her with her cloak. "Remember, I told you bed rest! I can very well see to my own cloak."

Abby clicked her tongue, ignoring the scolding, and swept the heavy, fur-lined cloak from Heloise's shoulders, gripping it to her chest as she took in the other woman's appearance. "You look striking, m'Lady," she sighed in her broad, Northern accent. "It should be you walking down that aisle."

"But the groom is my brother!" Heloise laughed, motioning for her cloak to be handed back over as she kicked the snow from her boots.

"Ah, you know what I mean," Abigail responded with a little pout, turning to retreat back to her bed with one hand supporting the heavy load of her pregnancy in front of her. "You would be a beautiful bride, Lady Heloise."

"If that's what it takes to become beautiful, I'd just as soon not," Heloise teased, taking quick steps forward to aid her charge as she eased back into her bed.

Abigail's house was little more than a hut, with partitions rather than walls separating the living quarters from the kitchen and reception area. The walls were lined with drying herbs and cleverly stored necessities, all framing the large bed at the center of the home that Abigail shared with her aging mother, and soon, her newborn child. There was no husband for Abigail Collins, nor was she willing to divulge the identity of the father of her child.

Though this distressed the township at large, Heloise understood completely. She couldn't tell Abigail, of course, but she had been in the exact same situation only a few years ago. There were many reasons why a woman might hold tight to such a secret, and all of them were valid.

The expectant mother herself was a slight thing, about half a head shorter than Heloise, with gleaming brown eyes and a short mop of curly hair to match. She had remained cheerful and lively throughout her pregnancy, seemingly unaffected by gossiping whispers and speculation. As far as Heloise was concerned as her midwife, Abby was the ideal charge, always eager to learn how to prepare herself and responsible enough to follow through on recommendations for optimal health during this delicate time.

"No Mrs. Collins today?" Heloise asked as she began to do her physical examination of the other woman's abdomen,

Chapter 3

pressing in to get a feel of where the baby sat within. "She is usually so invested in these visits."

"She's at the market, looking for curd tarts. Bless her." Abigail sighed, eyes following the progress of Heloise's freckled hands. "I've had an ungodly hankering for them of late."

"That is normal," Heloise assured her. "I've seen expecting mothers crave much stranger things. One woman repeatedly asked me if she might sample a bit of topsoil, as it was suddenly very appetizing to her."

"Mm, worms and all." Abby giggled, winning a smile from Heloise in return. She paused, tilting her head with a thoughtful glint in her eye. "You really do look lovely. I so rarely see you all primped and pinned like the lady you are."

Heloise scoffed, waving away the compliment, though she could feel a pleased warmth of color inching into her cheeks. She had made an effort to be presentable this morning, and not just to prove she had the capability to appear polished to her future sister-in-law.

She was wearing a mint green gown that she'd had made in the autumn, specifically for a large house party they'd hosted at Somerton. The fabric was perhaps a bit too light for a winter event, but it was, at present, the loveliest thing she owned. Besides, Heloise was no stranger to the chill of Yorkshire winter.

The seamstress had provided a length of broad ribbon in the same hue to wind into her hair, which her mother had assisted her with this morning. The contrast to her bright red locks was not so striking as to be garish, but provided a pretty enough contrast that she'd been given several compliments on the effect on the night they'd thrown the ball at Somerton.

She only hoped the style hadn't been interrupted by the hood of her cloak or the whipping of the wind as she'd ridden into the township on horseback. At the very least, she knew her color would be high and her eyes bright from the briskness of the weather.

She usually attended to her charges in simple clothes that she didn't mind getting rumpled or stained, but with the wedding taking place this morning, she'd had little choice but to ride in ahead of it if she wanted to check in on Abigail, who was due any day now.

"Have you had any cramping or the feeling of clenching about your belly?" she asked, satisfied that the baby was in a fully turned position. "The little one is ready to make a debut very soon. I need you to ensure that your mother will have someone ride to the dower house the instant you know it is time."

"Nothing as yet," Abby said, shrugging, "but I'm more than ready to have my body back to myself."

Heloise chuckled. "Well, I can't promise that will happen for a good long while. You'll still have to feed the babe and adjust to its sleeping habits, which will be erratic throughout the first year. You're in for quite a journey still."

"Well, aren't we always?" Abby grinned, her cheeks dimpling infectiously. "How about my feet, then? Is it normal for them to swell up like that?"

"Sadly, yes," Heloise replied, remembering her own penchant for simply going barefoot toward the end of her pregnancy. "They will return to a normal size after the babe is here, but they might remain a slight bit larger than they were before." *That was the case with me*, she thought, wishing she could share these things with someone other than her mother.

"I will craft some soothing oil at the clinic if you like, and you can ask your mother to rub it into your ankles and knees. It won't shed the swelling, but it will help with the discomfort."

"That sounds lovely." Abby nodded, moving to the corner of the bed with the intention to stand and walk Heloise to the door.

"Bed!" Hel commanded, brandishing her finger like a stern school marm. "Rest is essential now that you're close. Don't make me tattle to Mrs. Collins."

"Ah." Abby laughed, flipping her hand in the air. "You'd never do something so cruel."

"Best not to test that particular theory," she replied with a lift of her eyebrows. "I've been known to resort to extreme measures to get my way."

She retrieved her cloak from the peg where it was hanging, still a bit damp around the fringes, and wrapped it around herself. "I'll bring the tonic for your feet 'round tomorrow, unless that baby of yours decides to arrive just as we count down to a new year tonight."

Abigail patted her belly, aglow with that singular pink sheen that seemed to grace pregnant women. "Out with the old, in with the new, eh? Maybe the babe will take it to heart."

"Perhaps," Heloise agreed. "My brother and his bride-to-be certainly have."

---

*B*oudicea, Heloise's beloved bay mare, was tethered just outside of the clinic, a mere two doors down from the Collins abode.

Though it was only a short walk to the church from here, and Boudicea would be perfectly content on her own for a few hours, Heloise untethered her and led her along the pathway toward their destination. She imagined her brother Gideon would burst a blood vessel if she attempted to return to the manor on horseback while the rest of the congregation respectably piled into various carriages.

The cold seeped in through her cloak, raising a prickle of gooseflesh along her arms and legs while the snow crunched beneath her feet and Boudicea's hooves. Perhaps she had been earlier than necessary, she reflected, taking in the perfect silence of a morning in the township, blanketed in fresh snowfall.

It was because of this preternatural silence that the booming call of her name from across the path nearly startled her out of her own skin. Boudicea even gave a whinny of irritation, stomping a few steps backward in protest at the interruption of their serene promenade.

"If that isn't my darling Heloise!" a man's voice rang out, ricocheting off the wooden walls of the cottages about them. "I could see that hair from ten miles out!"

She smiled, amused despite the way her heart was racing

from the start he'd given her, and raised a gloved hand in greeting. "And I you, dear Sheldon, for you tower above all else!"

Sheldon Bywater, Marquis of Moorvale, chuckled and propped his hands on his hips. His legs were naked as the day he was born under an intricately folded Moorvale tartan of gold and blue. He'd grown out his beard for the winter, as he'd done every year since Heloise was just a little girl and he a raucous youth, always setting out to get her brothers into mischief.

His smile shone bright white against the black bristle of that beard, his hair already in disarray from the strength of the winds. As soon as Heloise crossed the cobbled path, he scooped her into a tight embrace, the warmth of his welcome drowning out that seeping feeling of frosty chill that had been permeating her cloak only moments earlier.

"You ought to wear your hood up, so you don't catch fever!" he chided, setting her back and examining her like a fretting matron. "You've not even a bonnet to protect your wee ears in this cold!"

"And there you are flashing your bare calves for the world to see?" she scoffed back. "Let he who is without sin cast the first stone, you shameless man!"

He laughed heartily, the volume of which seemed to ring out around the homes of the villagers. Almost as though to answer his disruption, a pile of snow slid off one of the roofs and landed with a splat on the ground.

"Shall we walk to the church?" Heloise suggested, urging Boudicea forward and taking Sheldon's arm before he could think to offer it to her. "I can't help but notice the absence of your shadow. Wherever is Echo?"

"At the church!" He chortled to himself, patting Heloise's hand as they walked. "I wanted to take a turn around the village and see it coated in white and that bright-faced curate was already half trampled under the old girl, lavishing her with ear scratches. He assured me he would look after her for a few moments while I took in this fine, fresh air."

"Sheldon Bywater, you are the only person I know who seeks to walk around in freezing temperatures," Heloise replied, a fondness in her voice.

"Well, I'm the only Scot you know, then!" he boasted, his brogue seeming to take on a more aggressive lilt at the declaration. "You come up to Hawk Hill for a season, lassie, and we'll see you married off good and proper, to a lad with strong enough stock to match you. I wager you'd love getting lost in the crags of Moorvale."

"I very likely would," she granted. "Though I'm not so sure about hunting for a Scots husband. I'm quite enjoying life as a spinster midwife, all things considered."

"It is a queer path for you to choose for yourself, to be certain. I imagine the folk here feel a little strange being waited upon by a Somers, no?"

Heloise considered it, tilting her head in thought. "You know, I haven't much thought about it. For the first year, learning under Meggie, I mostly attended to Rose while she carried little Reginald. When we took to the village for a few cases here and there that Meggie had picked up during her tenure, I would ask the expecting mothers to simply call me Heloise, rather than my Lady or Lady Heloise or what have you, but they all staunchly refused, and so I've learned not to fight it anymore. The township didn't have their own midwife, so I haven't displaced anyone, and I do not charge for my services, which surely is seen as a boon to some families, don't you think?"

"Oh, I wouldn't know," Sheldon responded with a dark sort of sobriety to his tone. "Women are mysterious creatures all, so far as I'm concerned. 'Twas merely curiosity on the part of a friend."

"Are we friends, at last?" She giggled, raising her free arm to wave to the assembled party standing outside of the church. "I recall for many a year, you only had time for Gideon, and then eventually Alex. I was never let in on the fun. I believe more than once you called me a 'wean' and instructed me to return to my nursery."

"I never!" he grumbled, his cheeks red with guilt. He cleared his throat gruffly and picked up his pace, tugging her along across the street. "Look alive, lassie, lest we miss the whole affair!"

She laughed merrily, allowing him out of her grasp so that he might flee to the safe embrace of masculinity alongside her brothers as they alighted the Somerton carriage. Alex looked very fine this morning in his new tails. The vibrant red of his hair was tamed into some semblance of respectability beneath a top hat, and his handsome features were molded into what appeared to be a permanent smile.

"Viscount Somers!" the vicar called as he burst from the church entrance. "Come in, come in from the cold! It's a sight warmer within! We lit the fires early, just for this joyous occasion!"

Reverend George Halliwell was a charming fellow in his fifth decade, with permanently rosy cheeks and a modest little potbelly that always stuck out from his robes. He had endeared himself to their community over the decades as a constant beacon of positivity, who was known to occasionally slide the odd jest into his sermons and to provide moral counsel with the care of a doting grandfather, rather than a stiff-backed judge.

As he ushered the group within, Heloise spotted a second carriage arriving, likely carrying the bride and her parents within. She paused at her work of handing off Boudicea to the family driver to watch it approach, the wheels of the Blakely family carriage squeaking on their hinges as they turned.

"They wanted me to ride with them," Lady Rose Somers commented, drawing up to Heloise's side with her son perched on her hip, "but I convinced Glory it was bad luck to have anyone but the bride and her parents in the carriage for the final moments of her maidenhood. I'm fairly certain she knew I was lying, but she wasn't willing to risk the off chance I wasn't."

Heloise giggled as the carriage came to a halt, turning to her sister-in-law and little nephew, only to remember her own instructions just two days prior.

"Oh, Rosie, I told you not to carry him in your condition," Heloise scolded, holding out her arms for the child, who was more than happy to fall into the embrace of a new and willing servant. "That's a good boy, Reggie. Come here."

Chapter 3

"Hel!" Reggie squealed, immediately moving to sink his fingers into her carefully arranged hair. "Hel Hel!"

Luckily, it only took a few encounters with the lad to develop lightning-fast reflexes, and Heloise caught his hands playfully and tickled his sweet little belly instead, winning a happy chortle from the boy.

Rose smiled at them, sliding a hand over the newly visible proof of her second child beneath her gown of plum and gray. The deep purple ribbons of her bonnet emphasized the roundness of her cheeks when she smiled, and despite Heloise's best efforts to be stern, she found herself returning the grin anyhow.

"Let us go inside," she suggested. "I imagine lingering in the frost isn't ideal either, hm?"

"Well, it isn't," Heloise grumbled, adjusting the weight of her nephew until it felt right. "He's going to be too big to carry before long!"

"Why do you think I'm still doing it?" Rose pointed out, holding the door open for them to draw within, where indeed it was much warmer and more pleasant.

Heloise had to set Reggie down on the ground (to his great offense) in order to shrug off her cloak and hang it on one of the pegs by the door. When she turned to retrieve him again, he had already toddled off at an unseemly speed toward his indulgent grandmother, who was assisting little Callie out of her new coat on the other end of the room.

As always, Reggie Somers acted without a care in the world for whether or not he had permission to do such a thing, and was received enthusiastically by those he had chosen to bless with his attention.

Heloise chuckled to herself, peeling off her gloves to stow away in the pockets of her cloak, taking in the congregation as it had developed thus far.

The housekeeper, steadfast Mrs. Brenda Laughlin, had herded the members of the household staff who wished to attend (and were not otherwise occupied preparing the opulent wedding breakfast that was to follow) into a section of seating near the stained glass windows. She had worn her best dress, a stiff blue linen that complemented her robust Celtic features quite beautifully. She had bought a matching bonnet specifically for the occasion, after much grumbling that she had missed Lord Gideon's wedding entirely.

It was amusing to Heloise that their actual mother, Ruthie Somers, had reacted almost in opposition to Mrs. Laughlin. She'd praised Gideon for his expedient and frugal elopement as the plans for Alex's upcoming nuptials became progressively more elaborate.

"A wedding on New Year's Eve?" she'd moaned. "How ridiculously indulgent!"

The bride, as it happened, had already intimately acquainted herself with the entertainment options available in the towns and cities near Somerton. She had ensured that announcements were sent to every major publication in Britain, as well as two shipped all the way to the United States. She had overseen the banns being read both here and down in Devonshire from which she hailed, and had agonized for well over a week about

Chapter 3

whether the wedding cake would have an almond or a sugar glaze.

It was a delicious sort of irony that starched and proper Gideon should have the unorthodox, scandalous wedding, while mischievous, fly-by-night Alex endured the rigorously traditional and respectable path. Anyone who knew her brothers would have immediately assumed that things would unfold the other way 'round.

"Lady Heloise, you are looking radiant," came a smooth, pleasant voice from the entrance hall as the town's handsome young physician, Dr. Richard Garber, entered the church. "I imagine knowing your own wedding day must loom somewhere near on the horizon must provide an additional thrill on a day like today."

Heloise shook her head, a little smile playing about her lips. "You will not convince me to give up spinsterhood, Richard. It has treated me far too well. And besides, you'd lose your one and only colleague on this cold and isolated moor."

"Ah." He shrugged, the gray of his eyes sharp in the late-morning light, and offered Heloise his arm. "If you'd marry *me*, we could continue to work together, could we not?"

"Hm," she said, taking his arm and allowing him to lead her toward the pews. "I suspect you might treat a wife somewhat more carefully than you treat a colleague."

"Alas, we will never know for certain unless we test the hypothesis, my dear Lady Midwife."

This was not the first time he had made such comments. They always came under the guise of having been a jest, but with enough flirtation in his tone to suggest that the offer was sincere, should she wish to take it. She released his arm and gave him a little nod as she took the second of the family pews, behind her brother and sister-in-law, at their seats at the front of the church, and did her best to disregard the way he bowed and let his gaze linger upon her before finding his own seat elsewhere.

It wasn't that Dr. Garber wasn't attractive. He was certainly handsome enough, with a fashionably sleek build, a head full of glossy brown hair, and gentle, practiced manners. He was intelligent and friendly and would likely make a very fine husband. Heloise had even allowed herself to consider it once or twice, though all the particularities of her situation generally dissuaded her from that line of thought.

"Do you see that?" Gideon asked, turning from the pew in front of her, his eyes sparkling with amusement. "He's got the dog sat on a pew like a person! It's a wonder he didn't try to affix a hat to her head."

Indeed, to their left, Lord Sheldon Bywater, a distinguished soldier and peer of the realm, was positioned next to his bloodhound, who was perched politely on the pew next to him while he absently scratched at her neck. Perhaps the truly remarkable thing was how little attention it drew from the other congregants.

"That's why he's still a bachelor," Rose commented. "He hasn't got room for another woman in his life."

"If I were a few decades younger, we'd just see about that," Ruthie Somers whispered, ushering the children into the pew between herself and Heloise.

"Oh, Mother, please," Heloise tutted, instinctively placing a

Chapter 3

hand on her daughter's curly head, as though to protect her from her grandmother's bawdy sense of humor.

Ruthie gave a wicked little grin and a shrug of her slender shoulders, her chestnut-brown ringlets quivering with the motion. "I am still young enough to regard handsome men, Heloise. So are you, for that matter."

"Mother!" she hissed, though her voice was drowned out by the pipe organ thrumming to life under the agile fingers of the young curate.

The atmosphere within the sanctuary buzzed with sudden excitement as Reverend Halliwell and Alex Somers took their places next to the pulpit, both men serious and upright as the doors opened to reveal the bride.

When she was a girl of sixteen, Heloise had believed that Gloriana Blakely was the most beautiful girl she would ever lay eyes on in her life. Even now, well into their second decade of living, she still believed it, watching the ethereal glow around the other young woman as she made her way toward the sanctum.

In those days of fiery youth, Heloise's resentment of Glory's stunning good looks and natural social graces had led to anger, dislike, and a not insignificant number of pranks at the other girl's expense. Today, she simply found herself stunned into perfect stillness as this incredible woman, who had once been such a thorn in her side, floated into the church on her father's arm, swathed in silver and white. Whether she was stunned by Gloriana's beauty or by the shock of her own sudden feelings of happiness upon seeing this particular person, she could not say.

Gloriana clung to Sir Reginald Blakely's side, though she

was a touch taller than her father. They had the same platinum hair, though Sir Reginald's was sparse and untamed while Gloriana's was a wealth of perfectly styled curls, arranged artfully into a wreath of holly and winter berries, with curls that tumbled down to frame her heart-shaped face. There were snowflakes embroidered into the gown she wore, flashing with silver thread as she made her way down the aisle. All the time, her pale blue eyes were locked upon Alex Somers with an expression of overt adoration.

It wasn't until the pair had passed Heloise's pew, with Glory's gown brushing against her fingers, that Heloise snapped back to reality. She settled into her seat, reminding herself of the occasion, and took note of her brother's face, his expression of awe at the approach of his bride.

As they reached the pulpit, Sir Reginald kissed his daughter's cheeks and whispered something into her ear that made her smile and blink away a welling of tears. He clapped Alex on the shoulder and the two exchanged a smiling nod before Sir Reginald turned and made his way back down the aisle to his own wife, who received him with a tight embrace and rested her head upon his shoulder.

What must it have been like, Heloise wondered, to grow up with parents who loved one another so openly? She stroked Callie's hair, a tendril of guilt blossoming in her soul for the things her child could never have, for the things that she herself had never had in the tender years of her life.

Alex and Gloriana clasped hands as Reverend Halliwell read from *The Book of Common Prayer*, instructing them to love one another and respect one another and honor one another and so on. It didn't appear the bride and groom really heard any of it, though they repeated the words well enough.

Heloise suspected that Gloriana Blakely had rehearsed her own vows in front of a mirror at length, perfecting her delivery and the advantages of this posture or that tilt of the head, to ensure the moment was utterly perfect.

And so it was.

She would want to recount it in copious detail for her friends and perhaps some enemies as well. Heloise had been surprised that Gloriana agreed to a wedding in the country in the dead of winter, which guaranteed a small congregation made up of only those who lived locally and her parents, who were perhaps the only Britons willing to travel nearly the full span of the nation through Yuletide.

Perhaps, she realized with a little smile, her impatience to be married to Alex outweighed her instinct to capitalize on even such a large opportunity to leverage her social clout.

It was an open secret that Gloriana had already been wearing the ring that Alex slipped onto her finger today, for quite some time. It was an heirloom that belonged to a great-grandmother on the American side of the Somers family, a pretty bauble of clustered gems that carried a legacy of true love. Heloise supposed that today's ceremony simply transformed the ring from a symbol of promise to a sacred bond.

Just like that, they were husband and wife. Gloriana Blakely, childhood nemesis and flouncing foe was no more. Now there was Lady Gloriana Somers, a sister.

When Alex gathered his new bride into his arms, he kissed her thoroughly enough that even the reverend raised his eyebrows. Those gathered amongst the pews reacted only with enthusiastic applause.

From the corner of her eye, Heloise was certain she saw Sheldon Bywater dabbing tears from his cheeks as he watched the proceedings.

As the congregation stood to shower the newlyweds with congratulations and cheer, all of them eager to join the delegation back to the house for refreshments and entertainment, Heloise lagged a little behind, watching the church as it emptied.

She leaned down to retrieve a sprig of winter berries from the aisle, which must have fallen loose from Gloriana's hair as she'd passed by. She held it up to the light streaming in from the windows, admiring the vibrancy of the red against the chill that nurtured it. The miracles of the moor and the beauty it created, despite its harsh edges and its ferocious storms and gales, never ceased to inspire a thrill of wonder in her heart.

"Auntie," came a sweet, soft voice from the doors.

Heloise looked up to see her daughter haloed in the purple and silver light of a winter's day, gazing at her from the end of the aisle. "Yes, my love?"

"Granny says you must come or we'll all catch 'fluenza," she recited, fidgeting with her skirt.

"Well, we can't have that, can we?" Heloise smiled, taking long steps to the back of the church, where she retrieved her cloak and offered her hand to the little sweetling. "Besides, the sooner we get back, the sooner we can try some of the wedding cake!"

Chapter 3

"Cake?" Callie replied, her dark eyes wide with eagerness.

"Mhm, and all sorts of other treats too. Come along, let's get to the coach before Granny turns into a snowman!"

Callie giggled, gripping Heloise's hand with the tight enthusiasm of a child who knows nothing but her own wants. Together they exited the church and joined the procession.

4

Caesar was the first honest-to-goodness purchase Callum Laughlin had made with his newfound, albeit humble fortune. A four-year-old stallion of mottled gray and white, Caesar had been described by his seller as restless, irritating, and insatiable for exercise—which was to say, perfect for Callum's needs.

A horse that was desperate for running and built for wide-open spaces was exactly the remedy to Callum's own impatience to be home.

Of course, prior to coming into Callum's possession, poor Caesar had been forced to endure being called Sugar-snout, after the distinctive spray of white on his nose. It was an overall undignified and improper name for such a fine mount. Changing his name was the first of many gifts this horse would experience as his existence evolved from a future of shambling stagecoaches to a horizon on Yorkshire, with endless wild land to run upon.

The business of his soon-to-be-executed gelding went

Chapter 4

unspoken. Callum thought it best that Caesar never know what they were going to do to him.

Bundled up in his warmest clothes beneath a layer of scarves and blankets, Callum had torn across the snowy terrain headed north, making triple the time he had been making in those stuffy, crowded stagecoaches. As one fellow traveler had commented to him, back near Stratford, attempting to get anywhere during the Twelve Days of Christmas was always going to be a busy affair, full of people who were trying to get to family in time to share in some of the festivities.

The military had made Callum respectful of deadlines, however, and he had told himself back on the southern shores of England that he wanted to be home in time for the new year. And so, he and Caesar had arrived on the fringes of the estate of Somerton, overlooking a frosted gate and the looming crescent shape of the manor house in the distance, with many hours to spare before the year turned over anew.

With a scarf wrapped so firmly about his face to protect from the frigid wind, Callum had to content himself with giving Caesar reassuring pats to the neck and scratches to the mane rather than telling him of all the wonderful things that awaited him just there, within their grasp.

It was a shame that Niles, the old stable master, had retired and moved south. Callum would have very much enjoyed showing off this fine example of horseflesh to the man who instilled within him a love of all things equine. At the very least, his mother would fawn and coo and say all the right things, even if she couldn't tell a plow nag from a destrier.

Heloise would love him, though. He grinned to himself,

beneath the layers of his bundling, at the thought of her comparing this young horse to her beloved bay mare, who had long been the finest mount for miles around. Would she begrudge Caesar his speed and beauty opposite her beloved Boudicea? Perhaps she had enough room in her heart for both.

His heart was thundering in his chest as he urged Caesar over the snowy field, toward the stables that he'd once thought of as home. It wasn't the speed nor the cold nor the exhaustion of so many days on the move that ignited him so, but rather the anticipation of finally having come to a moment that he'd imagined a thousand times for so, so long.

It was a bright day, but the clouds that hung in the sky were silver and fat, promising another layer of glistening powder in short order. Somerton was glorious in any weather, a glittering jewel on a hill amidst the most stunning scenery in Yorkshire, but Callum thought there was something particularly otherworldly about it covered in white with a stark, shining sun above.

He was breathless by the time he reached the stables, his blood surging hot in his veins. He held his breath without meaning to as he descended from Caesar's back, almost as though he couldn't quite believe his feet were about to touch home soil once again. Well, through a layer of frost and hay, anyhow.

He unwrapped the scarf from his face, breathing deep the brisk air and scent of the stables. He supposed there was something telling about his low breeding that he reveled so in the smell of a hayloft and a not indistinguishable undertone of manure, but ah, it was home.

Chapter 4

"Hello?" a thin voice called, a tawny head of hair poking out from the loft where Callum had once made his bed. "Who's there?"

"Callum Laughlin," he called back. "Here to see my mother."

"What!" the lad cried, as though this news were a revelation on par with the Second Coming. He tumbled directly over the side of the loft, scaling down the ladder like a squirrel on a tree, his cheeks just as puffy and his eyes just as bright. He couldn't have been more than ten years of age and was a complete stranger to Callum, which made it all the more confounding when the boy breathed, "Is it really you?"

"Afraid so," he replied with what he hoped was a reassuring smile. "Is my mother about?"

"No one's here, sir, Lieutenant, sir," the boy announced, his eyes darting from Callum's face to Caesar and back again. His accent was markedly more Highland than Yorkshire. "Everyone's in the township on account of the wedding. Sir. Lieutenant."

"Wedding?" Callum repeated, a chill taking hold of his lungs that had nothing to do with the weather. "Who is being wed?"

"Lord Alex is taking a wife, of course," the boy replied. "It's been in all the papers. Even in America!"

Oh, thank God.

"And who are you, might I ask?" Callum inquired, perhaps more tardily than was strictly polite, even if this was only a child.

"I'm Robbie," the boy said, puffing up his chest. "My papa is the driver and stable master here!"

"Is that so? Well, if you know who I am, then you know I was once the stable boy myself."

The boy nodded enthusiastically, his thoughts pouring out of him so fast, he had to gasp for breath between each statement. "Yes sir, Mrs. Laughlin reads your letters to me if I ask nice enough. Is that your horse? He's a fine one! Is he friendly?"

"He's tired," Callum said, patting Caesar's neck. "Might I trouble you to give him a nice brush and some oats? He's had a very long journey."

"Yes, of course, sir. I mean Lieutenant!"

Callum handed Caesar's reins to the boy, chuckling at his clear enthusiasm. "Is there somewhere I might wash and change while I await my mother's return, Mr. Robbie?"

"Oh." The boy flushed, his cheeks glowing pink. "Just Robbie, sir. Please. My parents are at the wedding on account of the carriages, but I reckon you could use our house if you please."

"I would very much appreciate it," Callum said with true and earnest gratitude. If he had time to rinse off the dirt of the road, perhaps run a razor over his jaw, and dress like a gentleman rather than a vagrant, he was sure he would make a more presentable impression on Heloise and her family as they returned from Alex's nuptials.

It was difficult to imagine Alex Somers a married man! He really had been gone for a long time, hadn't he? He couldn't fathom what type of girl had finally snared the rapscallion, unless of course he'd caved to the stern demands of his elder brother and simply picked a mousy miss who wouldn't complain too much about his conquests and capers.

He made his way into the renovated crofter's hut that sat behind the stables and began the process of peeling off his cold, damp travel clothes while the young lad insisted on heating up water for a bath. The little ragamuffin might look like a stable hand, but he clearly had the disposition of a cherub to go to such trouble.

How the Somers family had ended up with a Scottish driver and his brood was a story Callum very much looked forward to hearing.

The last he'd seen of House Somers was on a mild spring evening in London, four years past, at the moment that the reserved and calculated Viscount Gideon Somers had decided, shockingly, to elope with a pretty, curvaceous thing that he had apparently snatched up from a ball.

Rather than using Callum, who was still rather inexperienced at managing carriage horses on the road and navigating the greater part of Britain, the couple had decided to swap drivers with the Marquis of Moorvale for a swifter, more guaranteed passage to Scotland, where a legal elopement could take place. After all, Moorvale was known for the quality of his stables.

It had been his window of opportunity, hadn't it? Sheldon Bywater was not what most would imagine when thinking of a marquis. He was large and loud and quite a lot of fun, and it was he who suggested Callum depart with him to the Continent for a spot of soldiering, phrasing the suggestion as though it were simply an invitation to a corner pub for a pint and a laugh.

The marquis had taken a liking to Callum, who was still green and eager as a lad of almost twenty. He'd sponsored Callum's commission and for the first six months on the Continent, he had been on hand with the same regiment as a mentor and role model for all military life ought to be.

Callum had always believed he was destined for more than a life in service, scraping to the whims of those born to nobility, but without the benevolence of a nobleman, he wasn't sure he'd ever have found his way to the destiny he'd so wanted and the means to build a future he relished building toward.

Luckily, his rucksack had kept his belongings dry and as wrinkle free as could be expected after such a journey. Everything he owned was in a bag light enough to wear around his middle, but the fact that such things could belong to him was enough to spark a confidence within him that he'd never have known otherwise.

He did not linger in the bath, though the temptation to soak in the warm water until night fell was a strong one. He dressed hurriedly, not wanting to miss the return of the wedding party, and mentally promised he'd have a good shave and a proper washing of his hair on the morrow.

He tended his appearance in a mirror made of hammered steel, attempting to smooth his cravat and make some sort of sense of his hair. Even with the stubble, he thought he presented a reasonably tidy visage, particularly in the clothes he'd bought before leaving Paris. His dark blond mane was a little longer than he'd come to prefer it, but that could be dealt with later as well.

Would the Somers siblings see him as a new man, proved in the war and refined in the Continent? Or would they always see a stable boy who had dreamed of something more than his station?

What would his mother see?

He inhaled deeply, shaking these thoughts from his head and straightening his spine. He slung the sack back over his shoulder and stepped outside, back into the blinding white expanse of the winter.

Before he reached the stables again, he could see them coming. First as little black dots on the horizon, then as distinct carriage and horse shapes, a train of merrymakers coming over the hill. From here, he couldn't tell which carriages held the *ton* and which held the staff. They would have to get much closer for him to make that distinction.

"Mrs. Laughlin will want to see you straight away!" little Robbie insisted, taking the rucksack from Callum as though he were a proper guest to be waited upon. "You should go to the drive to await the carriage train. She'll be so happy to see you, sir. I mean Lieutenant. She missed you terribly."

"The drive," Callum repeated, knowing that the lad was right.

It seemed that he would not get to decide who he saw first, nor how or when, for all of the Somers household was coming toward him at speed, and he could do nothing more than stand and await them.

5

She knew.

Somehow, before they'd even made their way through the gates of Somerton or passed over the vantage of the hill, she knew.

Something in the air changed, a chill that hadn't been there just a moment before, an edge to the wind and a strength to the sunlight that sent a rush of nervous energy seeping through her skin and into her bones. She'd swear until her dying day that she had known, before she could have possibly seen him there.

"Is everything all right?" Rose had asked, her lips turned downward in concern, big golden eyes searching Heloise's face, taking in an expression that must have bordered on nausea.

Gideon mimicked his wife's frown, regarding his sister across the carriage with his customary air of seriousness. "This had better not be about Miss Blakely joining the family, Hel," he chided. "I thought we were past all that nonsense. I won't have you in a snit on their wedding day."

Heloise clicked her tongue in annoyance, the automatic instinct to snap at her brother dampened by the sudden and intense sense of foreboding that had overtaken her. Something was different, and she could feel it about her person like the crackle one is said to feel just before lightning strikes the very spot where they stand, but she couldn't very well say so to the two of them.

"I'm perfectly happy for Alex and Gloriana," she replied as evenly as she could manage. "I simply have quite a lot on my mind today. I need to prepare for the arrival of the Collins baby amidst all this hubbub."

"Mm," Gideon grunted, disbelief reflecting in his eyes.

For all Gideon's glaring and muttering, at least he was silent about her midwifery. She knew he wished her to be more a proper lady, even if he'd never say so. He was a good sort in that way.

Rose, for her part, was openly supportive of it, and even commented that she had seen Abigail a few days past in the village, and that she was looking very well. There was not a hint of judgement or disapproval about her tone when speaking of the unwed mother-to-be, though Heloise supposed that might have been because she herself was in the carriage and Rose was one of the few people in the world that knew the truth of Caroline's origins.

The only person, in fact, that knew the whole truth.

The carriage was moving slower than usual, careful of the slickness of ice on the ground, and Heloise thought the stunted pace would drive her completely mad. On horseback, she could have already made it to Somerton and back three times by now! Instead, here she was, being interrogated by her prig of a brother while her sister-in-law looked at her with the type of concern one usually reserves for death beds.

She held her brother's eye with a steady, if not belligerent stare, until he finally sighed and looked away, gazing out the window as they dragged along at the pace of a wounded tortoise. Heloise believed that if she put her mind to it, she had time to count every branch on every tree they passed within a reasonable accuracy at their rate of movement.

"Who's that there at the house?" he said, tapping one of his manicured fingernails against the carriage window. "One of the entertainers for the breakfast, you reckon?"

"No," Rose replied, leaning over her husband to take a look for herself. "Any staff would know to go to the servants' entrance. Whoever that man is, he is waiting for us to return."

"It's probably just one of Gloriana's other fiancés," Heloise said flatly, the indifference in her voice cloaking the way her heart had surged up into her throat and settled into a rapid, thumping chaos in her chest. What on earth was the matter with her?

Neither of her companions bothered to respond to her jest, instead choosing to lean on one another for a moment to get Rose re-situated in her seat, still adjusting to the weight of the growing child within her

She did her best not to fidget as they drew nearer to the house, finally able to pick up a modicum of speed on the well-trodden drive. If her nerves were already on edge to begin with, they frayed at the seams when the carriage in front of theirs ground to a halt, forcing their own to suddenly stop amidst the sudden ring of raised voices coming from without.

Never one to tolerate a lack of order in any facet of his life, Gideon immediately pushed the door open and leaned his head out to demand an explanation.

There was a flash of movement in shades of light blue as someone from the leading carriage alighted with sudden ferocity and lifted her skirts to race across the remainder of the driveway toward their mysterious guest.

It was then that Heloise began to put into words what her soul had sensed from the road. If she could have stopped Gideon from speaking as he drew back into the carriage, she would have, but it wouldn't have changed anything. All she could do was sit there, as though time were suspended around her, and wait for him to say the thing she already knew was true.

"That was Mrs. Laughlin," he said with a little crook of his lips. "It appears young Callum has finally returned from the war!"

Heloise saw the way Rose's posture straightened, the way her eyes snapped from her husband to Heloise. There was nothing to be done for it but to meet her gaze with a helpless shrug before her brother returned his full body within and pulled the door back into place so that the carriage might continue to its intended destination.

When it had finally ground to a halt, she awaited their driver, Graham, to wrench the door free for Gideon to emerge, despite his thorough demonstration just moments before that he was perfectly capable of operating the carriage door himself, then Rose, whom Graham took special care to help down as she supported the weight of her pregnancy with her other hand.

It felt to Hel almost as though she were not in control of her own body, like somehow she was watching from a distance as the Heloise below forced herself to scoot to the appropriate end of the bench and push herself up and out, allowing Graham to grip her gloved hand as she took a little leap to the frosty gravel below.

Her hood was still down, having had no reason to be drawn back up over her hair if she was riding within the carriage, and as such, unfortunately served as an extremely visible beacon in any crowd, particularly on a winter's day.

Still, she managed to see him first, through the muddle of people, still being held on either arm by the enthusiastic grip of his mother. He was smiling down at her with such a heartbreaking glow of joy that for a moment Heloise thought she might crumple directly onto the drive.

"There, now," Rose whispered in her ear, somehow managing to give her a body to lean into while appearing to require support herself. "Keep your chin up. We'll get you through this."

"And here I thought your invitation had gotten lost in the post!" Alex Somers cried, approaching with his smiling bride's hand clasped in his own. "Wonderful timing, Laughlin. Allow me to introduce my wife ..."

Heloise remained frozen stiff, stuck to the spot where she'd been standing as though roots had sprouted from her boots and twined into the earth below her feet. It was as though she had no control over her body and was forced against her will to watch Callum Laughlin exchange pleasantries and greetings with her family, unable to do anything to stop it. She was unable even to rouse herself to feign disinterest when she saw those dark eyes scanning the crowd and landing, finally, excruciatingly, upon her.

Alex was still jabbering away, with Gloriana and Mrs. Laughlin engaged in their own little tête-à-tête regarding the impending breakfast and how Callum *must absolutely* join the Somers family for the occasion. None of them seemed to notice the way the planet itself seemed to quake in that moment, though Heloise was certain it had.

He looked somehow like a different person entirely while still being exactly as she remembered. Those eyes, just like Caroline's, were so dark, they were almost black. The intensity of his gaze awoke a flash of heat in her body that managed to finally melt the grip of ice that was holding her in place, speeding the world back up to its normal pace around her as she felt her weight give into the support of Rose's body at her side.

"Come on," Rose murmured in her ear, guiding her toward the entryway of the house, just strongly enough to give Heloise the strength to tear her eyes from his, to blink quickly away the well of moisture that brimmed at her lashes and to step quickly and meaningfully over the threshold into her home, with her past, for at least one stolen moment, firmly behind her.

———

*A*lways the quick thinker, Rose spoke a few words to the nannies, and both Callie and little Reggie were whisked away to the nursery before the festivities could begin. No one seemed aware that the children might otherwise have been included in the breakfast, and so no one noticed aught amiss with the change.

Of course, little Caroline Cunningham wouldn't know Callum Laughlin from Adam. All the same, Heloise believed that one source of anxiety at a time seemed prudent, given the shock she'd just had, and any risk of someone making the connection was one she couldn't currently contemplate.

All one had to do was look into Callie's eyes to know she was his daughter. There was no hiding that, no matter whose name she bore.

As for Heloise herself, she knew that while she could not immediately flee back to the dower house, she would not be regarded with overmuch suspicion if she made an early departure, especially as she'd mentioned the impending arrival of a new baby in the township just before everything had been thrown into chaos. The only person present who might inquire as to the nature of her business this afternoon would be the doctor, and he certainly would ask her in private if his curiosity was piqued. After all, the man never turned down an opportunity to speak with her in private.

The wedding breakfast was held in the parlor rather than the dining room, to accommodate musicians and several tables adorned with a variety of finger foods. Seating was arranged throughout the room, and Gideon insisted that both Mrs. Laughlin and her son join the family in this double occasion of happiness.

At least with his mother present, Callum couldn't make a beeline for Heloise, though she could feel his eyes on her as she aggressively buttered her croissant, making a point to keep her back to the congregation as she tried to find the right phrasing with which to plea to heaven to make this pain swift and without consequence.

As though her guardian angel knew what she was about, in burst Sheldon Bywater, his voice booming over those of everyone else gathered, in excitement to see his protégé returned from the war. He stomped past Heloise, who had frozen in place, butter knife lifted like a conductor's baton, to avoid visibly wincing at the intrusion.

"Callum, m'boy!" Sheldon called, flinging an arm over the younger man's shoulders and giving him a hearty embrace. "I knew you'd do well for yourself, didn't I? I told Gideon as much too when I wrote to him of your commission."

"I believe you said there was nothing to be done for it now, as the letter would have arrived sometime after the deed was done," Gideon replied dryly. "And then you offered me your driver in replacement as though he were chattel."

"Aye, that I did," Sheldon replied happily, all rebuke lost upon him. "I suppose Graham might be expecting to return to Hawk Hill now that Callum has returned."

"Mm," Rose murmured. "Best of luck proposing that to him."

From her periphery, Heloise gathered that most of the family had clustered about Callum and Sheldon, enjoying the amusement of the reunion. She did not dare turn her head to search for a place to sit for fear that she'd be beckoned over by some well-meaning fool who didn't know the agony she was in.

Sir Reginald Blakely, the father of the bride, had taken a seat near the window and was presently gazing out upon the vista while he sipped on a cup of tea. This was a man who seemed very much content to simply sit in congenial silence if that is what the situation called for, and as such was perfect for Heloise's purposes.

She marched decisively over to him and took the chair opposite his, flashing him a smile she hoped did not appear overly awkward.

He returned the smile, a little twinkle in his eye that could sometimes be shared by two people amidst a moment of absurdity, and went back to sipping his tea and enjoying the sunlight streaming into the room.

How such an agreeable, pleasant man had produced a daughter like Gloriana, Heloise had never been able to figure out. She supposed it might have taken an indulgent parent to rear a spoiled child, however. While it was true that Gloriana was miles more pleasant than she had been during their years at finishing school, she still had a streak of haughty self-assurance that certainly had not been inherited, at least not paternally.

From her chair, she glanced over at the wedded couple, seated just a touch away from the remainder of the crowd, nestled into one another and whispering, as though they were perfectly alone.

Gloriana's silver dress shone like a mantle of diamonds in the afternoon light, her face tilted up to gaze into Alex's eyes with a staggering amount of raw affection. Perhaps when someone was born so utterly, devastatingly beautiful, she could become haughty on her own accord, with no contribution from her upbringing whatsoever.

Her heart hurt to watch them, so in love, so unconcerned with the world around them. It wasn't envy exactly, nor was it purely the function of some altruistic affection lurking within her. For a very short time, many years ago, she had believed she would have a future that looked somewhat like that, and she supposed that what she felt was both the pleasure one takes in witnessing something beautiful and the pain of knowing it is beyond your own grasp.

"Your friend the marquis is a rather loud fellow, isn't he?" Sir Reginald commented, his tone friendly if bland.

It startled Heloise, her eyes dropping immediately to her hands, as though she'd been caught looking at something she shouldn't. Now that it had been pointed out, she could hear Sheldon's voice again, spinning a raucous yarn about Callum's deeds of heroism on the front.

"... So, that's when young Laughlin here goes storming back into the barracks, covered in soot and gunpowder, and drags the colonel out by his elbows! All the while, the man was clutching that bottle of gin and sobbing about some bird named Yvonne, kicking his feet out like a toddler who'd been put to bed too early."

"It wasn't quite so fantastic as that," Callum demurred.

Heloise could hear the blush in his tone, the sudden discomfort with this attention. Had he always been so humble? She could have sworn she remembered a brash young man who would have puffed out his chest and reveled in such praise.

"Nonsense," Sheldon guffawed. "That's why he got that commendation, and a promotion to boot! *Lieutenant* Laughlin, in under five years! That's nothing to sneeze at."

"Lieutenant, you must stay with us in London this spring when you receive your medal," Gloriana said, her fingers winding absently through her husband's as she spoke. "Alex has been offered a position as a junior attaché and will be taking up residence in Mayfair in a townhouse that will have plenty of additional room."

Sir Reginald chuckled into his teacup, his shoulders bouncing and cheeks pink with amusement as Callum sputtered an attempt at a gracious reply.

"It took her less than a month to secure that assignation for her new husband, you know," he said to Heloise. "That boy has no idea what sort of life he's got ahead of him just yet."

"Well," Heloise replied evenly, despite the way her heart was still stuttering beneath her dress. "I've certainly warned him thoroughly enough."

Sir Reginald laughed outright at that, setting his teacup down and smoothing his pale blond mustache with his napkin. He propped his elbow on the arm of his chair and considered Heloise, his blue eyes sparkling with merriment.

"You're much more pleasant than she ever would have allowed me to believe," he said fondly. "Prettier too. Though I suppose you might've grown into it over the years."

"Oh, yes," Heloise confirmed. "It wasn't until a year out of Mrs. Arlington's that the scales fell off my cheeks and the snakes gave way to human hair. I still have to file my teeth down on a regular basis, in fact."

Chapter 5

"Oh, I can barely tell," he assured her with a pat to her hand.

"It's the residual hissing," she joked. "I can't seem to silence it."

Strangely, she could swear she felt a lightening of her concerns, as though the voices behind her had faded away for just a moment, allowing her to breathe. She couldn't rightly thank the man, for he had no reason to believe anything was amiss, but all the same she was appreciative.

"Glory would have been better served befriending a girl like you, rather than making enemies," he commented. "Before she met you, she genuinely did not know that the world would not always cater to her wishes and thank her for the privilege."

"I was beastly, really," Heloise said with a grimace. "Jealous and childish. I'd take it back if I could."

"I wouldn't," Sir Reginald countered, raising his eyebrows for emphasis. "You taught her resilience and that not every girl must follow the path laid out in front of her. You made her question her choices and learn to navigate discord. I cannot say how important those things have been to my daughter, especially as my paternal teachings were sorely lacking in these subjects."

"You seem like a wonderful father," she assured him. "I wish mine had been half so kind."

"Mm, luck of the draw, that." He nodded, not bothering to coddle her with empty platitudes nor false acclaim for the late Lord Somers. "Still, you've grown into a remarkable woman. It is not many ladies of the *ton* who would not only reject being debuted, but learn a trade and practice it! You needn't money nor shelter nor occupation, and yet you perform a momentous task in your little township with true devotion and enthusiasm. You are a singular woman, Lady Heloise, and you should be proud."

"Proud?" she repeated, stifling a surprised hint of laughter. "I rather think my scandalous choices and confirmed spinster status have given my brother gray hairs before his time."

"That one was born with gray hairs," he said with a wink. "You know, I often imagined what you must be like, having only the lens of Glory's tragic tales to go by. I pictured a girl much like my own daughter who took to life with fire and brimstone instead of smiles and charm like Glory or a caretaker's serenity like Rose. In a way, I feel like I knew you then, all those years ago."

"Perhaps you did," Heloise suggested. "In your own way, of course."

"Maybe so. If that is the case, then you must allow me an indulgence."

"What's that?"

Sir Reginald smiled, leaning back in his chair. "Allow this sentimental old man to be proud of you, Lady Heloise. Consider my pride a proxy, just until you can come to see yourself the way I do."

Heloise bit her lip, the strangest sensation to cry rising up in her throat. "Thank you, Sir Reginald," she said softly.

"Of course, of course," he chuckled, waving his hand as though it were nothing at all and craning his neck around to survey the progress of the breakfast. "Now, when is that blasted cake coming out, hm?"

6

The arrival of the wedding cake finally gave Callum a moment to breathe.

In a sudden gust of activity, the attentions of the gathering shifted from what Callum considered a soft but firm interrogation of his whereabouts for the last several years to rapt attention on the cutting of the cake by the bride and groom.

Only his mother remained, standing at his side with a reassuring hand on his shoulder while the gathered *ton* flowed around them to their new destination of interest: a white table already outfitted with gold-edged china on which the guests would sample the wedding cake.

It was surreal standing in this room as a guest, knowing one of those plates was meant for him. Yes, his mother was here too, though he genuinely wondered if she would have returned belowstairs if not for his arrival. The head of the household staff is still a servant, after all, no matter how long she'd lived with a family.

To make matters even more uncomfortable, Lord Somers

had extended an invitation for Callum to stay at Somerton for as long as he liked—that is—in the house proper, *not* in the servants' quarters. He had been rescued from the necessity of having to give an immediate answer by the arrival of this sugar-glazed monstrosity that must have consumed several pounds of eggs, butter, and flour.

It had been a very long time since he had last laid eyes on Alex Somers, and though he looked much the same as he had before that first departure to Oxford so many years ago, Alex must have changed a great deal to have ended up engaged to the woman standing next to him. This was no mousy miss to be kept complacent in a country house while Alex carried on with his wild ways. This was a beauty cut from glittering ice and diamond, with the calculating eyes of a chess master complementing her pretty face.

Meeting her eye gave him the sensation that she could pluck all of his secrets right from his mind and stow them away for a time when she might find them useful. It was unsettling, to be certain, even if it didn't feel particularly malicious. Perhaps he was simply paranoid from his years abroad, being forced to remain on guard no matter how desperately he wished to relax. Yes, that must be it. It was absurd that he should find himself sizing up the prowess of a young bride on her wedding day.

As for Lady Heloise, she seemed to be doing her utmost to avoid having their reunion until they could be alone. While of course he could see the wisdom in such a precaution, especially with how high emotions would likely be running once they could properly greet one another, it was a true torment to see her sitting there, not so very far away from

Chapter 6

him, and be unable to stride over and pull her directly into his arms like he wanted to.

He had done his best not to gawk too obviously, though he imagined anyone who was paying close attention would have found him utterly transparent.

She was resplendent. She glowed in a shaft of sunlight, her body wrapped in a silk gown of pale green and her hair as bright and glossy as it had ever been, wound about her head with a burst of matching green ribbon. The Heloise he remembered preferred her hair down her back and her clothing more suited to durability than style, but it was, after all, her brother's wedding day.

Her eyes were a darker green than that gown. He hadn't been able to see them up close in several years, but he remembered them as well as you remember the smell of the ocean or the taste of fresh-baked bread.

She had risen from her repast with an older gentleman near the windows to view the cake cutting, illuminated in glorious backlight as the sun cast burnt orange and pink hues onto the room, beginning its journey below the horizon so early in the day that it made the winter feel even chillier.

"Won't you have a slice of cake, Lieutenant Laughlin?" the Viscountess Somers asked him, startling him so suddenly out of his reverie that he had to stifle a gasp.

She was a pretty little thing, lush and curvaceous with big, golden eyes that blinked up at him with an earnest warmth. Her lips were curved in a friendly smile, or perhaps a little show of amusement at having caught this stranger staring at her beautiful sister-in-law.

"Thank you, Lady Somers," he managed, accepting one of those fine, fragile little plates from her, along with an equally delicate fork. "We met once before."

She looked far more composed today than she had on that night, some years past, when she had eloped with Gideon Somers and left Callum with the Marquis of Moorvale, changing his life forever.

"Yes, I recall," she replied with a smile, lowering her lashes at the memory. "I'm afraid I was rather distracted that night and did not make the appropriate introductions at the time. If you'll excuse my rudeness, I am very pleased to make your acquaintance now, and I hope we might still be friends."

Friends? A viscountess wanted to be his friend! He stumbled over what he hoped was a gracious reply, his head swimming with this new and strange world that was somehow living in just the place where he'd left his old one.

"Tell me," she said, balancing a delicate bite of cake off the edge of one of the silver forks. "What are your plans now that you've returned to England? Or have you decided?"

He blinked at her, caught for a moment like a doe in the crosshairs of a hunting musket. Well, he couldn't tell her everything, could he? Not without Heloise giving her consent to his plans. He couldn't outright lie either, when he was hoping to marry into this very family.

Instead, he decided to attempt an abridged version of the truth, clearing his throat and attempting a confident tone. "I will sell my commission in the spring, and hopefully have enough revenue together with my savings to purchase a small home somewhere in the country for myself and my mother."

Chapter 6

"Oh," Lady Somers said, raising her eyebrows. "I did not realize Mrs. Laughlin would be leaving us."

"I haven't mentioned anything to her yet," he said quickly, a nervous heat rising beneath his skin. "I would ask you not to mention it to her until I've had an opportunity to make sure the idea is a feasible one."

"Of course, yes," she agreed, though her expression had a hint of concern to it where it hadn't before. "I hope you will be staying with us for the remainder of the winter. It is my assumption that searching for a property to purchase will be much more amenable come the spring."

"I'm sure you are right." He sampled a bit of the cake on his plate, only to immediately regret the explosion of sickly sweetness that overtook him as he attempted to keep his expression as neutral as possible.

"Yes, I agree." Lady Somers sighed. "Heloise and I told her the almond glaze would be less abrasive, but Glory loves sweet things and wouldn't hear it once she had made her choice."

At the sound of her name, Callum instinctively glanced over his shoulder, to the last place he'd seen Heloise standing, only to find a milling of people he did not recognize making conversation over slices of the wedding cake.

"Has Lady Heloise gone?" he asked, putting on his best tone of nonchalance. "She never did like to stand on ceremony."

"It isn't that," Lady Somers told him, those eyes of hers sparkling with a keenness that suddenly made Callum feel quite exposed. "She has duties in the village to attend to as a midwife and will likely wish to freshen up and rest before returning for tonight's New Year celebration. You will join us too, I hope?"

"Midwife," he repeated dumbly. "Did you say Lady Heloise has become a midwife?"

"Yes, quite!" the viscountess replied happily. "She assisted with the birth of my son, Reggie, and has been overseeing the progress of my current pregnancy."

"O-Oh!" he stammered, shaking his head in embarrassment. He had not even realized the woman in front of him was with child, though now that he looked at her properly, he of course could see the way her dress had been modified to allow for the growth of her belly. 'Congratulations, Lady Somers."

"Thank you, Lieutenant," she replied. "Now, I must return to my husband's side before he becomes overwhelmed with the crowd. If you're looking for Lady Heloise, you might try the stables."

"Why would I be looking for Lady Heloise?" he asked, but the viscountess had already gone, crossing lightly over the sunset hues of the parlor's natural light as though she had not suggested anything at all out of the ordinary.

The sound of her voice found him first, drifting out over the eerie stillness of winter air from the interior of the stables. She was murmuring to one of the mounts, too low to make out the words, but it was her voice for certain.

It was unexpected to be affected so by something he had

never even considered a fundamental part of Heloise. She did not sing nor did she recite poetry with melodic intonations. She spoke without flourish and always said what she meant.

He had already taken in her vibrant beauty with his eyes, but hearing the timbre of her voice shattered something deep in his chest, something he had been keeping cold and solid to survive the years away from her. He wanted to pause, to linger in it for as long as he could, just to prolong the pleasure of rediscovering Heloise Somers bit by bit after so long away.

He edged around the corner of the stables and caught sight of her within, murmuring into Boudicea's ear as she secured the saddle on her back, rewarding the mare each step of the way from a wealth of sugar cubes concealed in her pale hand. She was wrapped in a cloak of russet brown, a fine thing rimmed in fox fur, with a pattern of leaves stitched through the back in a variety of earthy colors. If her hair had been down, it would have spilled down over the sagging hood in glorious red waves, blending into the autumn colors reflected so artfully in the cloak.

He could not help drifting closer, his boots crunching on the frozen hay beneath his feet, drawing her attention from her task with an elegant twist of her body, bringing that cloak around herself like a sheet of protective armor. Her skin shone alabaster white, those emerald-green eyes flashing against the light of the setting sun.

"Lieutenant Laughlin," she gasped, reaching up to swipe an errant curl of red hair from her forehead. "I did not hear you approach."

"Lieutenant Laughlin?" he echoed with a surprised chuckle. "Surely you know me well enough to sidestep formalities. Don't you, Heloise?"

She appeared to shiver, whether from the gusts of cold air seeping in from the outside or from his words, he could not be sure. Whichever it was, she appeared to recover herself quickly, drawing her arms over her chest to still her body and lifting her head and setting her jaw with a resolve he found all too familiar.

Seeing her like this, poised like a warrior queen, made his heart ache for the years he had missed by her side. With the low sunlight creating shafts of jewel-toned light from the rafters above, even the ribbon in her hair could have been an emerald tiara, pinned painstakingly into place as she rallied her knights for battle. She was spectacular to behold, but her posture was markedly defensive, and as such it gave him pause, the smile of greeting melting slowly off his face.

"Is aught amiss?" he managed to ask, his throat dry, heart suddenly clenched in a web of frost. He found himself taking a step forward, hand outstretched as though to offer some invisible tribute to the woman he loved. "Heloise, are you not pleased to see me?"

She released a tiny sigh, her breath escaping from her lips in a cloud of fog against the cold, and dropped her eyes to the ground, focusing on some mote of meaningless dust on the stable floor. She spoke with an air of disconnect, breathy and impatient. "It isn't that I'm displeased that you've returned safely, Callum. Of course I am glad you're home. It has simply been a very long time since we last saw one another, and very much has happened in that span of time."

"Naturally," he replied, a wariness lighting signal fires in his mind. He spoke with the steady voice he had learned to keep in the line of combat, a voice that betrayed nothing of the way his heart had begun to sink in his chest. "I wish to hear about every moment I missed."

She smiled without joy, reaching up quickly to flick a finger at her eyelashes, and shook her head. "It is far too late for that now."

"Will you not look at me?" he said softly, studying her face as she kept it stubbornly turned to the side. The sudden chill in his bones had nothing to do with the brisk weather. "After all this time, would you not grant me at least that?"

She squeezed her eyes shut for a moment, then set her jaw and turned her face to meet his. "Do you believe I owe you some sort of penance or gratitude?" she breathed, her voice dangerously low. "Do you imagine that I have been patiently holding vigil, having no idea where you'd gone nor why, and allowed myself to keep a candle burning for you with no indication whatsoever that you were doing the same?"

"You knew exactly where I'd gone and why," he returned, aware that his own impatience was beginning to tint his words. "And you know very damn well why I couldn't write you directly."

"Well, I certainly seem to have known a lot without realizing it!" She shook her head, reaching into her cloak and withdrawing a pair of gloves, which she fumbled with, giving her an excuse to look away from him as she drew them over her hands. Her voice was shaking now, though with anger or the onset of tears, he couldn't be sure. Knowing Heloise, it was likely the former.

"Hel, this is madness," he breathed, taking two quick strides over to her and reaching out to still her hands from their task, sharing the warmth of his own skin with the wind-whipped chill of hers.

She went very still, her eyes still fixed on her hands, which were now held within his, her chest rising and falling in time with the little clouds of warm air that emerged from her lips. "Callum," she whispered, as though it pained her to say his name. "Please, don't."

He studied her from where he stood, the curve of her face that she kept turned away from him, the rigid posture of her body beneath that cloak, and the coolness of her hands within his own.

"Something has happened," he realized, struck nearly dumb with how obvious it should have been to him from the start. "Something monumental."

She did not answer him, instead choosing to remain frozen perfectly still. It was almost as though she feared him, which of course was ridiculous. Heloise Somers feared nothing. Anything capable of frightening her would be truly fearsome indeed.

He dropped her hands, taking a step back, suddenly overwhelmed with horror at the idea that he was having this effect on her. "I left to build a respectable future for myself," he said quietly. "So that when I returned, I would be worthy of you."

"No," she replied, turning those eyes of hers up at him with such a sudden and intense ferocity that he was almost knocked off his balance. "You left for *you*, not me. I wanted you here. I was ready to marry you when you were naught but a stable hand, and you knew it. You left because the idea of letting my dowry support us wasn't good enough for you."

He opened his mouth to reply, outrage blossoming in his chest at this accusation, which was *entirely false*, but she turned her back on him before he could speak, gathering Boudicea's reins in her hands and throwing herself onto the horse's back. He was helpless to do anything but watch her kick forward, horse and woman lunging out of his reach as she burst from the doors of the stable, and out onto the expansive white lawn of Somerton, presumably in the direction of her duties and whatever other secrets had unraveled in his absence.

He found himself left behind, standing with an expression of befuddlement, exposed to the first whirls of snowfall as they blew into the stables, with only the strange and unfamiliar as options for his next destination.

He wondered if perhaps it might have been simpler, somehow, if he'd just stayed at war.

7

The truth of the matter, of course, was that Heloise Somers had no particular destination in mind when she'd spurred Boudicea out of the stables and into the endless white expanse of the Somerton grounds.

The wind bit at her face, ripping the hood of her cloak back and ringing in her ears as great bursts of snow exploded upward under her mare's hooves. To her credit, Boudicea seemed unconcerned with the frosty terrain and obeyed her mistress's need for wild abandon as though she could sense its necessity deep within her equine soul.

Perhaps Boudicea was more intelligent than any of them realized. Without much in the way of direction or command from her mistress, she led them to the dower house, slowing to a stop near the small, double-stall stable that she often lounged within when Heloise had taken her from the stables proper. She whinnied, tossing her head with a spray of caked snow flying off the strands of her glossy, brown mane and releasing something akin to a sigh as Heloise melted forward, clinging to her neck, as she pressed one frozen cheek to her horse's warm skin.

"I did not expect him to follow me," Heloise confessed, squeezing her eyes shut as she wrapped her arms around the sturdy, loving neck of her mare. "I did not expect him to wish for everything to resume as it was. Can he not see, as plain as day, that things are not the same at all?"

Boudicea did not answer, for she was only a horse. Still, the steady warmth and patience of her presence in the tension of this moment were more than many a human companion might offer, and when Heloise slid off her saddle, the horse turned to check that her mistress was all in one piece, nudging her affectionately with her broad, very cold nose.

By the time Hel had removed Boudicea's kit, given her a quick brushing, and filled her trough, the cold had seeped deep into her bones. For the second time that day, she reflected on the foolishness of wearing a dress commissioned for the early autumn to a winter wedding.

The dower house was dark, with most of the staff in the manor proper for the New Year celebrations. Still, there was a fire lit in the drawing room, so at least one of the staff had the same misanthropic disposition that Heloise herself possessed, else the poor sod had simply drawn the short straw on the odds that Lady Heloise would be adopting the position of recluse in the wake of a double holiday.

Everything she was wearing felt wet, somehow. Strangely, the driest thing of all was the cloak, which she supposed was likely due to the merit of its material rather than some preternatural phenomenon by which water passed straight through one cloth and into the one beneath. She left her boots by the drawing room fire, hanging her cloak there as well, and made haste up the stairs to her room to change into something a little more sensible for a time of year when the world seemingly lost its pulse.

The ancient Greeks, which her teachers at Mrs. Arlington's had been so very fond of, believed that it was a mother's love for her child that caused the turning of the seasons. Demeter, the goddess of the harvest, mourned to see her only child wed to Hades, and thus, banished to the underworld. When Persephone was with her husband, Demeter grew so listless and despondent that she failed to rally the warmth from the sun and the green from the earth. Everything grew as dark and cold and bleak as Demeter herself, until finally the gods agreed that Persephone could come to live with her mother for half the year, just so that the crops might grow and the sun might give warmth once again.

At the time, she had thought Demeter histrionic and controlling. After all, her own mother had moved back to America when Heloise was still in knee socks and hair ribbons, and neither of them had ceased to thrive, had they? Why couldn't Demeter simply write amusing letters to her daughter and have them sent via courier over the River Styx for half the year? Yes, it all seemed rather dramatic and unnecessary, and a young Heloise had much preferred the goddesses of wrath and fury, who raged against pain rather than found themselves crushed by it. Hera, she recalled, had been a particularly engaging figure.

She chuckled to herself, drawing a heavy green gown from her wardrobe that would serve both to protect her from the elements in a more significant way and to not require her to restyle her hair for the New Year festivities this evening.

Chapter 7

Callie was still scarce bigger than a babe in arms, and far, far off from one day being taken away in marriage by some man who might very well live as far away as Hades itself. Still, every year, when autumn began to settle, and the world turned colder by the day, Heloise would think, for just a moment, that Persephone must have departed back to her marital bed, and left her weeping mother behind in a field of ripe summer flowers that would soon turn gold and brittle, crumbling to dust under an eventuality of snowflakes.

Since becoming a mother herself, she had found far more compassion for poor, mourning Demeter, who simply did not have the will to continue while her baby was deep underground, reigning over the dead.

In the days of her pregnancy, her own tumult of emotions might very well have turned the world cold and white, had she been given domain over such things. She had fled from Bath-Spa in the night, leaving most of her things behind at Mrs. Arlington's School for Young Ladies in an effort to reach Yorkshire as fast as possible. She had sent out three identical missives, explaining her situation, to all of her living family members.

It had been an unseasonably cold year, with the frost still clinging to the burgeoning blades of grass well past Easter. The necessity of bundling up under layers of fabric had been a blessing, hiding her condition for as long as she possibly could, until she knew beyond a doubt that she must go into hiding.

She arrived home ahead of both of her brothers, unsure if either one would come. She knew Callum was in London with Gideon, unable to receive any sort of letter without raising the eyebrows of his master. Even if he had been alone, she could not write to him about something this sensitive, which might be intercepted and read.

Oh, how she had dreamed of what she would say when he finally returned home, of how she could throw herself in his arms and cry into his strong, broad chest. She had plotted and planned meticulously, dredging up ways she might get him alone before having to face her family, negotiating the imaginary matter of their hasty marriage and what might follow.

Of course, nothing had played out the way she'd expected.

Alex had been the first one home, to her utter astonishment, and had set about the business of making sure her secret was safe with an efficacy that probably would have concerned her, under different circumstances. Gone was her blithe, frivolous brother who was never where he was supposed to be and certainly never behaved appropriately. In his place was someone who acted confidently and with speed. He dismissed many of the staff members for the remainder of the season, sent for a tailor in Leeds, as not to alert anyone in the neighboring area of her condition, and provided company entirely without judgement or admonishment. In fact, he had only ever addressed the pregnancy when asking if she was all right or to tease her as her body grew.

It was the first time Alex had seemed to her a man grown, all while she still felt the child thrust into an adult's world.

Gideon, of course, toppled her plans right over once he'd finally shown up. He had arrived home in the dead of night with some stranger driving the coach, married to another stranger, and had left Callum behind in London with Sheldon Bywater. The next she heard of the father of her child had been by chance, standing next to Mrs. Laughlin as she read a letter explaining his departure for the war.

Heloise had stood helpless on the lawn, heavy with child, and unable to react to the horrific news she was hearing for fear of giving away her baby's paternity. She had felt the blood drain from her face while Mrs. Laughlin read the letter, sobbing madly and proclaiming that her son would be slaughtered on the battlefield for certain. That moment and her near collapse was what had given her secret away to Rose.

It was the one time in her life she'd come close to fainting dead away. Even when she'd given birth to Callie, amidst blinding pain, she had not felt as helpless as she had that night on the green, as all of her remaining hopes had been dashed to dust in the cool night air.

Had she given up on the dream of Callum then? No, likely not. She must have held on to a glimmer of hope that he'd return to her, at least until after she'd named her child after him. Caroline, she'd decided, so that she might be called Callie for short. Some part of that decision had come from the fear that he might never return from the war at all. After all, many men did not, especially those who were not fortunate enough to be amongst the gentry and given safer orders.

She sighed, glancing at her bed, so lush and inviting here in the middle of the day. If she must needs return to the manor to ring in the new year, it would be the last time this winter. Just one party and afterwards she would be free of her obligations to be in the manor proper and near Callum Laughlin.

She could survive that much.

Just one night. She could manage it.

She crawled into her bed and tucked her feet under the dry, heavy material of her skirt. She was asleep before she could decide upon what dreams she might like to have.

The New Year at Somerton had become quite the festivity in the years since Gideon had wed.

Gone were the somber nights where the staff was set free to find their revelry in the township while the Somers siblings were content to have a solitary glass of port and a vague conversation about their plans for the coming year, often retiring to bed well before the toll of midnight.

Rose d'Aubrey Somers had turned Somerton into a palace of cheer and well-wishers, bringing with her all of the traditional New Year celebrations she'd grown up with back in Devonshire. While most years they observed the traditional course of picking a king and queen of the new year from amongst the staff and gentry alike, this year it was unanimously decided that the bride and groom deserved the honor.

Alex and Gloriana, still in their wedding finery, had been placed at the head of the massive banquet table that was usually kept in the ballroom for storage, while the entirety of House Somers, including all of the staff from the dower house, gathered around to share in food and festivity until the clock struck midnight. For this one time of year, there was no social rank and order, and all were equal and welcome.

There was an irony in tonight being the night that Callum chose to return home. Their difference in status had ever been the wedge driven between them, hadn't it? Even as children, called in for dinner from their play, and shunted suddenly and with firm hands in opposite directions for the evening.

Callie and Reggie had not protested at being put to bed early, for they were still adrift on the high of Christmas day, and were placated with one final present to say goodbye to a year well-lived. It seemed that the universe still smiled upon Heloise in the matter of keeping Callie away from her father until she'd figured out how she was going to address the situation. She rather suspected that this docility at being put to bed on New Year's Eve was in its final year or two, at least insofar as Reggie went. Her own daughter, to everyone's utter shock, was an obedient, shy little girl who always did as she was told.

Ruthie, their grandmother, had once commented that heaven must have gotten it mixed up, with well-behaved Caroline acting much more like her uncle Gideon in his childhood, and wild child Reggie channeling his auntie Hel. Gideon had agreed, but had also commented that if he'd survived Heloise's childhood, he was likely better prepared to go through it again.

Heloise knew very well that her best route of action tonight was to put on a smiling face and endure the evening, hoping that the hours might pass quickly and midnight would come and go in the blink of an eye. She'd have to stay tonight in the manor house, lest she raise the suspicion of her family, but tomorrow she would flee back to the dower house with Callie in tow and remain there until the first blush of spring. She would stay firmly and totally outside of the manor house until Callum Laughlin was gone and she was once again free to resume the comfortable routine of her life. It would be easy, with the temperature and ferocity of the snow a happy excuse to keep her comfortably enclosed on the other side of the grounds for as long as necessary.

She had long lamented that Rose knew her secret, but in this, at least, she could consult a confidante. It would mean Rose continuing to keep secrets from her husband, but if she hadn't told him by now, Heloise trusted she had no temptation to do so. It would only be a matter of finding the time and privacy to consult her sister-in-law and gather her advice. How much worse this would all be if she were utterly alone in her secrecy!

Callum Laughlin was, of course, at the table. He was seated with his mother near the bride and groom, looking utterly devastating in a gentleman's kit. She had never seen him dressed so, with a glossy, tailored suit cut to the broad and healthy lines of his imposing frame and a starched cravat folded against his throat. Heloise had only ever seen him in work clothes (or nothing at all, of course), and found it difficult not to stare at this presentation of nobility in a boy who had once chopped the firewood in nothing but his breeches just a few yards away from where they now sat.

Even his speech seemed more refined, somehow, though she was careful not to reveal that her ear was turned to his voice, desperately curious to hear every word he spoke. He was appropriately humble about his exploits on the Continent, though he did not begrudge a pelting of questions from practically everyone at the table. He blushed more than once, lowering his coal-black eyes to blink away the shock of such attention, and sometimes smiled in such a way that Heloise thought her entire soul might shatter like a pillar of glass.

He looked across the table at her more than once, open longing in those dark, dark eyes. She did her best to avoid returning his gaze, though it was a difficult task, with how he drew the eye. He was still somehow cut from pure Yorkshire wilderness, even in a suit and cravat. He had cut his hair since she'd last seen him, which he'd been painstakingly attempting to grow so that he could bind it at his neck. Now it was short enough to brush his cheekbones if unstyled and loose around his face.

She flexed her hands under the table, blinking rapidly to dispel the memory of her fingers in his hair, of the smell of hay and grass that seemed to linger there, in the mussed tresses that were always warm from the sun. It would serve her no purpose to allow such memories to take hold of her, especially now.

Next to her, Dr. Garber did his absolute best to keep her amused and distracted. He chatted to her about the clinic and how they might improve and expand it in the coming year. He suggested certain books they might order from Cambridge, which he could retrieve the next time he was down. It was important to keep an up-to-date library, he told her, with all the most recent procedures and discoveries to integrate into the practice.

She was grateful for the distraction, and perhaps a bit more encouraging with Richard's flirtations than she might have otherwise been. She allowed him more than once to touch her hand, to lean forward and whisper in her ear, so close that his breath stirred the red-gold ringlets that framed her cheeks.

Her heart was racing and her cheeks were flushed, but it was not from the good doctor's attentions. She could feel Callum watching, almost to the point of heat from the dark embers of his eyes every time the doctor took a liberty or brushed too close. She didn't have to look up to know his lips would be drawn into a grim line of dissatisfaction. He had always worn his emotions clear as day on his face, with none of the *ton* artifice that she'd had to endure in the rest of her life masking his true feelings.

She had loved that about him. She had loved him.

If they had not been so careless, so brash and reckless and impatient, he might have returned from the war to find her unspoiled and worthy of a true courtship, if of course he still wished it. Part of her took a keen sense of pain-laced pleasure in the fact that Gloriana Blakely was at the head of the table, a woman so glowing and beautiful as to embody what a base-born man might think of a woman of Society. Next to her, Heloise knew she was a freckled troll, and it was best that Callum see it, at last, and know that the pedestal he had put her upon was not one that was deserved, but rather the result of a limited scope of the world.

She swallowed, instructing herself to breathe, reaching for her wine in the hopes that it might dull the flickering lights and shadows that were spinning ever more persistently in her mind.

As she came back to herself, she got the distinct impression that Dr. Garber was pressing his knee toward her legs, as though he was hoping to make contact beneath the table and through the layers of her heavy winter dress. Was she imagining it? She did not look toward him to confirm, instead drawing her ankles together so that such contact would be impossible. If he was disappointed, he did not show it.

He is only interested in you for your dowry. You are an easy target, the eccentric spinster sister of the Viscount Somers, close at hand and a burden on her kin.

She quaffed the remainder of the wine in her glass, closing her eyes to allow the heat of the drink to soak through her. She was never this dramatic. She must pull herself together. It was only a few more hours.

What else could possibly happen in such a short amount of time?

8

Silly as it may have sounded to an outsider, the way Callum felt that night amongst the Somers household reminded him strongly of his first days in the army.

It hadn't been so bad back in the dining room, when everything was set into place and the movement of the meal was enough to indicate how he should behave. Now that they'd moved into open space, where they might freely mingle, he was crawling out of his skin. He hadn't felt this awkward in years.

When he had been a green lad of twenty, traveling under the starry-eyed ignorance of what was to come, he had arrived in Calais wearing his common breeding clearer than any badge or medal pinned to a soldier's chest. Every word he spoke, every gesture and glance, gave him away as someone beneath even cursory notice from the officers, which would have been well and fine, had his conscription at the behest of a marquis and an officer besides not placed him outside of the reach of his equals at the bottom of command.

Chapter 8

He wasn't sure what had been worse, being ignored and disregarded by the gentry or being glanced at with suspicion and excluded from even the most mundane of interactions by his own ilk. There was nothing quite so painful as having been the cause of a bout of laughter dying if ever he drew too close.

Of course, Lord Moorvale had been more than friendly, and had done his best to provide a sort of guidance for Callum once they'd arrived at their destination, but for as much comfort as direct acknowledgement might have afforded him, the queerness of it seemed to sap it all away in the same breath. He could never have told any of this to Sheldon Bywater, of course, for it would have seemed ungrateful and childish, and for all of the little miseries, what Bywater had done for Callum had changed the trajectory of his entire life. It was a kindness that could never be fully repaid.

So it was much the same tonight at Somerton, with polite, if cool reception from those amongst the nobility who remembered him as a stable hand and direct avoidance and discomfort from members of the household staff, who had once considered him their peer. Once again, it seemed the only person in the room he knew how to approach was Sheldon Bywater, who was just as jovially oblivious to Callum's discomfort as he had ever been.

Even his own mother seemed to hover awkwardly near him, as though she had forgotten how to act in his presence in the years since he had last seen her. It was unbearable. It made him agonizingly aware of every spot he chose to stand in, every positioning of his body or tilt of his arms. He felt as though he, too, had forgotten how to exist within the context of home.

He was still numb from what had happened earlier, in the stables. Of all the ways he had imagined reuniting with Heloise Somers, somehow it had never occurred to him that she would have been angry at him for leaving. He thought they had understood one another perfectly when last they'd spoken. Had they not planned explicitly about building up to the type of stability that would make their proposed union more palatable to both of their families?

What a fool he'd been! He'd spent four years dreaming of her, every night, certain she was dreaming of him too, certain she was awaiting his return with the same limb-lost pain in his absence that he felt without her. All the while she'd been going about her life as though he'd never existed at all! Even now, she was pink-cheeked and smiling, nodding at something that predator of a doctor was whispering to her over glasses of champagne.

A nudge at his shins startled him out of his brooding reverie, his fingers clenching around the glass he held in an effort to prevent himself showing his surprise. He lowered his eyes, looking for the offending party, only to see a bolt of yellow fur winding its way through his legs and back out again.

"Nero!" he cried, dropping down into a squat to greet a creature he'd once nursed with clotted cream on the tip of his finger.

The cat wore a velvet ribbon of striking royal blue around his neck, and had at least doubled in size since the last time Callum had seen him. He purred heavily into Callum's outstretched hand, raspy tongue stealing a few rogue droplets of wine from the pads of his fingers.

The relief that swelled into Callum's chest at such a warm, enthusiastic welcome was almost too much. He felt the most absurd stinging at the corners of his eyes, and forced himself to shake away the sensation before he made an utter fool of himself. At least someone knew that Callum was the same person he'd always been.

"I'm afraid that cat no longer adheres to pesky norms like ownership," his mother said from above, drawing his gaze up to see her smiling fondly upon the scene. "He doesn't even know which building he lives in anymore, nor whose bed he prefers by night."

He cleared his throat, pushing himself to his feet and jerking down the line of his waistcoat, a bit of heat spreading across his cheeks at having made such a boyish display of himself. "I suppose a cat this handsome is entitled to indulging in his choices," he said with a crooked smile. "He certainly isn't a runt any longer."

"Mm," Mrs. Laughlin said, tilting her head with a bit of a sparkle in her dark eyes. "His mother still chases him out of the kitchen with remarkable success. She's half his size and twice as fierce."

"Ah, good old Bones." Callum sighed, a chuckle escaping him. "Protecting her kingdom at any cost."

"Well, any sensible woman ought to do the same," his mother replied, lifting her glass to her lips. "Once you know something is precious to you, all you can do from that point onward is hold it close and defend it from any who might take it from you."

Nero grew bored of this line of talk and darted over to the bride and groom, leaping easily into the bride's lap with the confidence of a feline who knew himself welcome. Indeed, the lady did not gasp or push him away, but only began to scratch him between the ears without breaking in her conversation with her new husband.

"It's strange to see them settled so," his mother remarked, watching the scene alongside him. "I never thought to see Lord Alex marry of his own accord, much less a woman like that one. Lord Somers, yes, I suppose, I knew he must marry eventually, but I'd make a poor fortune teller indeed. I never could have pictured a woman like Lady Somers at his side."

"It seems a good match, though," Callum said, seeking out the head of House Somers in the crowd, where he and his wife were standing opposite the township's Reverend Halliwell and the dowager viscountess. The group was exchanging what appeared to be pleasant conversation.

He noted that Gideon Somers had his hand resting affectionately on the small of his wife's back, as though such a thing were the most natural gesture in the world for a man who once feared to even laugh in mixed company.

"Oh, for certain, yes!" his mother exclaimed with an enthusiastic nod. "Just look around you! Do you ever remember ushering in the New Year in such grand style back in the old days? Lady Somers has breathed life into this drafty old manor."

"Yes, it seems she has," he agreed. "Perhaps Lady Heloise will be next to settle into wedded bliss?"

"Mm, don't be so certain." She drew his eye to meet hers, taking a step closer to speak at a lower volume. "That doctor has been chasing after her for months. I believe he even inquired with Gideon as to asking for her hand, but you know Lady Heloise is a wild one. She moved into the dower house when her mother returned from the Americas with a foundling babe, and seems content enough to live out the rest of her days there, if you ask me."

"Really?" He did his level best to keep his voice even, despite the spark of hope that flared up in his chest. "Lady Heloise may be wild, but she is also beautiful and wealthy. I find it a surprise that she survived even one Season in London without landing a husband."

Mrs. Laughlin snorted, perhaps giving away that the spirits had begun to loosen her command over her emotions. "There is a war on, my dear. There are far more available ladies of good breeding than there are eligible bachelors, and the competition is fierce. Lady Heloise can hardly be bothered to pin her hair up, much less coax and coddle some *ton* gentleman into asking for her hand." She paused, frowning as she considered the youngest Somers sibling, who had turned to allow Sheldon Bywater into her conversation with the eager young doctor. "Yes, there are the fortune seekers, but I rather think she sees right through them. I thought perhaps Lord Moorvale himself would ask for her hand, after seeing the way he's doted upon her all these years, but he spent the entirety of the autumn gathering moon-faced over some chit from the low country."

"Moorvale and Heloise?" Callum repeated, unable to disguise the horror in his voice at such a pairing. "It would be a disaster."

"Aye, it would at that." Mrs. Laughlin frowned. "Can you imagine the noise? I just like to see all the little ducklings home to roost, I suppose, but that Heloise has never gone where she's meant to go."

Callum laughed despite himself. "I hardly think the Somers family are wayward ducklings, Mother. They've proven that in spades, if nothing else."

"Well, perhaps I'm talking about you and not them," she returned with a little pout. "I suppose you might consider giving me a grandchild or two now that you're home and settled. Perhaps there's a girl in the township who's been awaiting your return?"

He shook his head, a fond half smile overtaking any discontent he might have been feeling at his current marital prospects. "I'm hardly settled. I've not yet been back a full day. I don't even know where I'm going to sleep tonight."

"Why, in one of the guest rooms, of course!" she told him in a tone she might use to give information to a simpleton or one of the chickens. "Lord Somers already told you that, surely?"

He grimaced, shrugging his shoulders. "I wasn't sure that was what he intended. It's damned awkward, isn't it? I don't want to be a guest in the same house where my mother is a servant!"

"And whyever not?" she demanded, narrowing her eyes and plopping her hands on her hips. "I do a right fine job with the running of Somerton, I'll have you know. You will never have a more hospitable stay in your life."

"I do not doubt it!" he said quickly. "But surely you do not wish to remain a servant for the remainder of your days?

You must bristle at the thought that they are placing my status above your own."

"They are doing no such thing, Callum Laughlin," she snapped. "Why would you say such a thing?"

"Mother, be reasonable. There is a clear divide between the servants and the gentry. If given the choice, no one would pick the former. In fact, it is my dearest wish to buy a property and take you away from daily toil, so that you might live out your life in comfort and ease."

"Comfort and ease?" she repeated, her words taking on a dangerously dark tone. "Is that the woman you believe me to be? A layabout who resents honest work?"

"I believe you've worked hard enough for several lifetimes," he answered, squaring his shoulders. "You can't tell me you don't wish to be done with all of the bowing and scraping that comes with a life in service."

"Bowing and scraping!" she breathed, her eyes glittering with fire. "Look around you, son of mine. All members of this household are here tonight, in one room, sharing wine and bread as the clock counts ever closer to a new year. Do you see bowing and scraping about you?"

"Mother, it's a special holiday," he began, pressing his lips firmly together at the way she held up the flat of her palm to silence him.

"It is, isn't it? And I plan to enjoy it!" She pursed her lips, looking at him in such a way that he felt he was a small child again, about to be scolded for his ingratitude and dirty cheeks. "You might consider doing the same," she suggested, then turned on her heel and stalked away, leaving him once again adrift in a sea of people.

He watched her go, the swish of her best blue dress blinking out of sight as she went in search of better company than his own. He wasn't sure if he was angry or frustrated or just sad. So far, he was utterly failing to reunite with the most important people in his life in the way he might have imagined.

He found his way to the refreshment table to top up his glass of wine. It was true that everyone was in the same room tonight, that master and servant were not a function of the revelry, but it was also true that when Callum scanned the room again, taking in the people assembled, they had divided themselves by their stations, keeping like to like, the way things always were.

When the grandfather clock in the hallway released its melodic chime of midnight, it drew a cheer of satisfaction from the assembled merrymakers. No night was ever quite so hopeful as the dawn of a brand new year.

Lord Somers raised his glass, calling the attention of all assembled to him, and he smiled. Callum was uncertain he'd ever seen Gideon Somers smile like that. It was startling. He suddenly seemed a young man, which of course, he was. It was only that Gideon Somers had ever worn the somber mantle of a man well into his years, and as such had always seemed so much older than his true age.

"We've completed another year at Somerton," he announced, "and have another just beginning. As my wife tells me is tradition, once again we will release the air of a bygone year into the world and welcome in the chilly breath

Chapter 8

of a brand new year! If you'll all accompany me, let's move to the foyer."

There was a rumble of anticipation, bright smiles, and eager faces as everyone poured out into the hall toward the foyer.

Callum allowed them all to go before he followed. After all, he wasn't sure where in the procession a man like him ought to stand.

The whole thing was curious bordering on strange. Of course, he knew this was a long-standing tradition throughout Europe, but he had never once seen it performed, least of all at Somerton. By the time he arrived in the foyer, everyone had fallen quiet, raising their glasses to one final toast of the year as Lord Somers strode to the heavy double doors that led from the manor into the drive.

He flung them open to a great cheer and a hearty blast of frosty wind, laced with a torrent of snowflakes, that curled its way into the foyer.

Everyone was so taken with the cheer of the moment, that for several suspended seconds, only Callum seemed aware that something was very, very wrong.

Gideon's face changed first, his eyes darting over to where his family stood. When he turned on his heel to rush out onto the drive, he was followed closely by the barreling bulk of Sheldon Bywater, and then a trickle of bystanders.

Callum, for his part, felt frozen in place. The smell was as familiar to him as the sun rising. It was as though the world around him slowed down, grinding second by second in a sickening, syrupy lurch. He was already moving, he knew, already spurred into action borne of years of familiarity with the tang of tragedy that hovered on the cold night air.

He parted those standing in front of him, making his way through the crowd with the elegance of a man who was accustomed to chaos. The sound of the men shouting on the drive was the only sound. The room had gone deadly still, captured in frozen uncertainty as the flurries of snow wafted in from without. It wasn't until he'd reached the front of the room that the world appeared to resume its usual, frenetic pace.

"Fire," shouted one of the maids, dashing back indoors with her hands to her cheeks. "There's a great pillar of smoke in the sky!"

"Where?" the viscountess snapped immediately, gathering up her skirts to march toward the door. "On the grounds?"

"Oh, my lady," the girl moaned, turning to face her mistress with tears glittering in her eyes. "It's the township that's ablaze. There's a great orange shadow on the horizon and the smell is something fearsome. Surely everything is burnt to ash already!"

9

Heloise did not have time to stand by whilst the details of an emergency response were negotiated.

The longer everyone stood around talking and arguing and panicking, the more a fire would spread, licking its path of destruction through the close-cobbled homes and shoppes of their beloved township. Somewhere in that chaos was a heavily pregnant Abigail Collins, who might have already inhaled dangerous amounts of smoke or worse.

She pushed past everyone, her glass of champagne discarded on its side in a pile of snow. Boudicea would take only a moment to be saddled and she could be off, able to provide whatever aid she could to the township. Her silk slippers crunched in the snow, the hem of her gown dragging in the cold wetness. She barely felt it at all, instead focused on the task ahead of her.

Did the township have an organized fire brigade? She did not know.

The stables were low lit and eerie in the night. Several of the horses were aware of the smoke, and were snorting and crowding in their stalls as the air filled with thick tension and unease. A piebald stallion she didn't recognize was pushing against his stall door, eager to be free of this flammable enclosure, lest the fire come any closer. Two of the geldings were tossing their heads, moaning in fear as the smell grew ever stronger.

By the time she'd led Boudicea out into the open and hurled her saddle onto her back, her fingers had begun to go numb. The task of securing the buckles and harnesses was far more difficult with stiff knuckles and chattering teeth, but she was too determined to stop and consider the wisdom of pushing forward.

If her brothers hadn't come into the stables at that exact moment, she might have completed her mission and gone tearing into the night with nothing but the clothes on her back to protect her from the brutality of a Yorkshire winter.

She didn't know how many times Gideon said her name before she heard him. To her, it seemed as though she were floating in a trance of pure instinct, aware of nothing but her goal, and the next she was shot through with discomfort and pain as the cold shot through her limbs. The only warmth was her brother's hands on her cheeks, as he said again, "Hel!"

She blinked at him, licking the dryness of her lips as her senses came back to her. "Gideon, I must go," she whispered, blinking up into the intensity of his gaze.

He was startled by her behavior, she could tell. His brow

was furrowed into deep rivets of concern and he still did not release her cheeks from his grasp. "Heloise," he said, the softness of his voice doing nothing to detract from the fact that his words were a command. "Go inside and put on your boots and cloak. Tell Alex what supplies to bring along and he will collect them immediately. Alex?"

"Here!" her other brother replied breathlessly. "Graham and Robbie are readying a few of the faster mounts. Dr. Garber will ride ahead with Sheldon and Laughlin. The rest will need to be managed by Rosie."

Gideon gave a curt nod, letting his hands slip from Heloise's cheeks to her shoulders. He looked hard into her face, as though he might suss out any lingering irrationality from the glint of her eyes. "Go with Alex," he said again, giving her a gentle nudge in her brother's direction. "Boudicea will be saddled when you return."

"Come on, Hel," Alex said, gesturing in the direction of the house.

Heloise followed, gritting her teeth against the pain in her feet as a thousand tiny needles of cold erupted with every step she took. Once they were inside and had sent one of the maids for Heloise's boots and cloak, Alex listened carefully to her instructions and turned on his heel to head back into the darkness with an alacrity that brought a little more alertness back into Heloise's limbs.

Later, she couldn't remember at all the process of bundling up against the cold, nor of retrieving her mount from the stables. It was as though in one moment she was looking into Alex's face and the next she was hunched forward, reins in hand, as Boudicea galloped breakneck toward the township, a single lantern swinging from the saddle hook to light their way.

The scent of burning wood reached much farther than Heloise would have imagined. She had not even covered half of the distance between Somerton and the township before her eyes and nose were stinging with the bitterness of it. She wondered, as she spurred Boudicea faster, how much of the flurry surrounding them was actually snow. It seemed to her just as likely that the ghostly white flecks that wove through Boudicea's mane and sprinkled along the threads of her cloak were the ashes of the things that were already beyond saving.

At some point, she had returned to that state of heightened necessity in which she could not feel the cold. She imagined that if she were still in her wet slippers, with bare hands and shoulders, alone on the path of snow and ice, that she might have felt much the same sense of disconnected calm that was grounding her just now. If Gideon hadn't come to stop her, she might have caught her death out here, driven purely by her primal impulses, without care for sensibility.

She would have been no good to anyone with frostbitten toes and an onset of hypothermia. Thank God for Gideon's utter and complete inability to be swept away on a torrent of irrational emotion.

She had expected to see a dull glow of raging red and orange as she drew nearer to town, perhaps with flames licking high into the sky as they consumed rooftops. Instead, a spray of glowing red embers seemed to mingle in with the snowfall, creating the kind of fearsome beauty that is reflected in all of the world's greatest dangers.

Chapter 9

The shouts of panicked people and the popping of wood as it split from heat and pressure cascaded over her, at once overtaking the steady thrum of hooves on earth. A curtain of smoke hung thick in the air as Heloise rode through the gates of the township. She had intended to ride directly for the clinic, where she might save valuable medicines and materials that they would surely need amidst this disaster. However, it was immediately clear that the clinic was at the center of the devastation, unreachable amidst the chaos.

"Lady Heloise!" called a voice from below, drawing her attention down in a snap of panic. It was elderly Mrs. Collins, her charge's mother, still in her night-rail with naught but a silk cap to keep her head warm in the snow.

Heloise slid off Boudicea without a second thought, reaching for the other woman's hands. "Where is Abigail? Is she hurt?" she demanded.

"She's in the house," she replied, panic raw in her throat, her eyes large and bright. "I wasn't strong enough to move her. Please, help us, Lady Heloise."

"Are my brothers here?" she shouted, squeezing tight to the older woman's fingers. "Did they arrive ahead of me?"

She nodded, seemingly too stunned in her shock to even cough away the smoke that curled around them. "The church," she said. "I saw Lord Somers at the church. He couldn't hear me calling. My daughter! Someone must help her!"

"Take my horse to the church and send one of the men to your house." Heloise glanced over her shoulder, in the direction of the Collins house, but could make out very little through the clouds of smoke and steam. She turned back to

Mrs. Collins with urgency in her voice. "I will meet them there. Go inside and be warm, or you will make yourself sick."

She handed the reins over, squeezing the other woman's hands and awaiting a sign that she had understood her instructions. As soon as she was given a hint of a curt nod, she spun on her heel and charged through the shroud of smoke, in the direction she knew the house would be. She lifted the neckline of her cloak up over her nose and mouth, ducking between masses of people who were either fleeing in terror or attempting to help others. The two were indistinguishable from one another in the thick of the panic.

She thought she heard someone call her name, though of course it was impossible to tell as she drew nearer to where the fire had burned the hottest. While there were still glowing ghosts of the fire that had raged here amidst the beams that still stood and the rubble on the ground, it appeared that the ferocity of the fire had been stamped out, either by the efforts of the townspeople or the aid of the snowfall.

Regardless of whether or not the fire was still burning, the smoke still had a choke hold on the town square, hanging in a cloud so thick that it was hard to keep one's eyes open, much less breathe the air. Hel forced herself to inhale through the cloth of her cloak, squinting through the acrid veil as she trudged onward, twice almost losing her footing to sliding steps. The cobbles were hard and smooth with ice that had formed from the snow on the ground having rapidly melted and then refrozen in a dark and deadly slick.

The Collins house appeared at last, though from this distance and in the dark, she could not tell how damaged it might be. What she did know is that smoke could be fatal to even a strong and healthy person if breathed too deeply, and Abigail at the end of her pregnancy was in a particularly precarious state.

"Alex!" she called, hoping her voice would carry through the confusion, that Mrs. Collins had stayed true in her task. She ripped down the cowl, so that her voice might project farther, and called again. "Alex! Gideon! I'm here!"

She stomped through the remainder of the terrain leading up to the little cottage, calling again and again as her voice went ragged and raw in her throat. When she reached out to turn the knob on the door, she cried out in pain, jerking her hand back as the heated metal sizzled at her hands. She bit down on her cry, looping the hand under the material of her cloak and forcing the knob to turn. She had to apply the full force of her body to get it open as the wood groaned and split in protest. When it finally gave way, she toppled forward onto her hands and knees onto the threshold of the home.

"Heloise!" the voice came again, somehow smothered beneath the ringing in her ears. "Where are you?"

"Here!" she cried, though she could not stop to find her way to that voice, not when Abigail was in here, possibly dying. She squeezed her eyes against the stinging tears streaming down the sides of her soot-stained cheeks as she crawled forward. She coughed to dislodge the heavy film of soot that coated her mouth and throat, feeling with her hands as she edged forward. "I'm here!" she called one more time, her voice little more than a hoarse whisper in her throat, and then, desperately, "Abigail?"

She could make out what appeared to be a human form, slumped in a heap on the side of the bed that Abigail shared with her mother. From this distance, she could not tell if the body had the tell-tale rising and falling of a person still breathing, only that it was cloaked in white and collapsed on its side. "Abigail!" she called, her voice breaking into little more than a rasping plea. "Can you hear me?"

In her focus on the other woman's limp body, she had not heard a second person enter the house. It wasn't until strong hands had wrapped around her middle, hauling her up to her feet, that she realized she wasn't alone in this dire, desolate situation. She spun, expecting one of her brothers to be standing before her, her arms already rising to embrace him with gratitude for finding her. It was too late to pull back by the time she realized that the man in front of her was Callum Laughlin.

"Callum," she breathed, her voice drowned under the cacophony of the night.

His eyes were dark and wild, his breath coming in great, heaving gasps. He had discarded the cravat and coat he'd worn at the dinner table, looking far more the man she remembered in an ash-smeared shirt that clung to the sheen of sweat on his body. She felt light-headed, like she was looking at a ghost, and forced herself to unclench her hands from where they were balled into his shirt.

He clasped her wrist, jerking his head toward the door to the cottage and turning to take her from danger. When she jerked her arm back, he spun in disbelief, looking fit to toss her over his shoulder if it meant getting her out of this house.

Chapter 9

She shook her head, taking two steps back and lifting her arm to point. She attempted to scream "Help her!" but realized that no sound came from her lips.

He looked over her shoulder, his eyes widening in alarm, and pushed her behind him, gesturing that she should leave the cottage immediately and wait outside. Any other time, she might have argued, but she found herself stumbling backward, desperate to once again draw breath from the open night, even one so bathed in the smell of ruin.

She stumbled out into the square, pulling the cowl back up over her face and forcing herself not to take great, gulping breaths of air. After all, even out here, the air was still thick with smoke. The blast of cold wind that swept between the houses was some small mercy, though there was little she could do to take advantage of it, frozen to the spot as she was with fear thick and terrible in her throat.

It only took a moment for Callum to appear in the threshold. Abigail was cradled in his arms like she herself was the baby, her head limp and resting against his chest. He burst from the cottage amidst another gust of smoke and sparkling flecks of fire-lit air, taking care with each step, as though he were not himself fleeing certain death.

"Abigail!" Heloise breathed, rushing forward to meet them. "Is she alive, Callum? Tell me she is alive."

He nodded, his face set in a grim mask that appeared completely devoid of emotion. He brushed right past Heloise, his pace keeping its same steady speed as he carried this woman to safety. He did not even look at her, instead keeping his dark eyes locked straight ahead, on the path to safety.

"We must go to the church," Heloise told him, scurrying to match his gait. She had to hoist the cloak and her skirts up in her fists to keep up with him, but she would not be left behind as her own charge was taken from her. If he noticed that she was struggling to match his gait, he gave no indication of it, set in his task with all the blank commitment of a gargoyle at vigil.

She told herself she was not hurt by being ignored as though she didn't exist, though his blank disregard had sent a pang of something painful ringing in her chest. It was silly, wasn't it? She did not want his affections. She cleared her throat, hoping that some of her volume would return as they passed into cleaner air, but still spoke in a strained, hollow little voice quite unlike her own. "Her mother is at the church," she continued. "And Alex is to meet me there with medical supplies."

Abigail's body finally seemed to give a shudder as proof of life, though she did not raise her head nor open her eyes. Her short brown curls, which had been clean and glossy this morning, were matted to her cheeks. Her face was bright pink from the heat and her lips cracked and bleeding. The first thing they must do once she was settled was to give her hydration and cool her skin down.

As the church came into view, Heloise was certain it was the first time in over an hour that she could breathe. She stopped where she stood, supporting herself with her hands on her knees, and stood stuck in one place, gasping in great breaths of cold night air as though she'd never had occasion to breathe before.

She did not know if Callum stopped or even noticed her

sudden absence, for by the time she raised her head, he had vanished into the chapel with Abigail Collins, and there was nothing left to do but hurry after him.

10

The inside of the church was a surreal change of scenery, bright and clean opposite the disaster just without. Callum's arms were burning at the dead weight of a heavily pregnant Abigail Collins, but he held her steady. When he'd seen her on the floor of that charred little cottage, he had been certain she was dead. From the first moment he could feel her ribs swelling with small, vital gasps of air, his heart had been in his throat.

He knew this girl. He had sipped ale with her in the summers of his youth, had tumbled her once or twice in a flurry of youthful abandon. Just now he could remember her laugh and the sparkle of her oak-brown eyes, but he couldn't think of the last time she'd entered his thoughts. It was a numb shock to find her as she was, swollen with child and on the brink of death.

When he'd found Heloise in that house, he had been filled with rage and urgency. His heart had been thundering, his ire aflame that she'd put herself in such senseless danger. He had stopped feeling anything at all when he realized that she had been risking her life to save someone else. It might have been her lying in a slump in a smoldering ruin, breathing in gulps of black poison. It might have been both of them, if he hadn't followed her.

Now that he'd reached the fabled safety of the church, he found himself frozen in place, uncertain what to do next. He held the unconscious woman in his arms, blinking at the makeshift triage before him, with only her weight and the pain in his legs to remind him that he was not dreaming.

"Lieutenant Laughlin!" called Reverend Halliwell, hustling over where Callum stood. The man was still in his suit from the party, his cheeks round and pink with exertion. "What a relief you've found Miss Collins. Please, bring her inside. Her mother has been beside herself!"

Callum nodded, certain he couldn't find any words to respond, and found himself trailing after the good reverend like a duckling follows its mother.

Lady Rose Somers hustled past them with blankets piled in her arms. The lovely bride of Alex Somers was kneeling in her silver gown, showing a gathering of children how to cut strips of old linens for bandages. His own mother was holding a baby, rocking it with soothing words while the mother sobbed silently beside her.

None of it felt real.

"Here we are," Reverend Halliwell said, gesturing to a pile of sheets and a pillow near the pulpit. "Mrs. Collins and Lady Somers have been preparing for Abigail's arrival."

The dowager viscountess stood, shaking dust from her skirts, but Mrs. Collins stayed where she sat, tears brimming in her eyes as she awaited the delivery of her daughter to this humble bed.

Callum lowered her as gently as he could, uncertain how one should position a woman so heavy with child. As he got her settled into the sheets and began to withdraw his arms, her eyes fluttered, opening for just a moment to fix on him. Her mouth moved, as though she wanted to say something, but just as quickly, she appeared to faint again, her head lolling to the side like a doll's.

"Thank you, sir," Mrs. Collins moaned through her tears, placing a hand to Abigail's head. "Thank you for saving my girl."

"We are in your debt, Lieutenant Laughlin," the dowager said, placing a hand to his arm. "You saved two lives in one."

He nodded, uncertain what he could possibly say. He glanced down at Abigail as her mother began to clean the soot from her cheeks, and got the urgent desire to flee into the night.

"I must go back out," he said to Ruthie Somers, who withdrew her hand as though it were keeping him from his duty.

"Lady Somers, I was hoping to take a census of those we know are safe," the reverend said, stepping into the space at her side. "Perhaps you can assist me? After all, you are very good with names."

He turned just as Heloise came hurrying in their direction, her arms filled with supplies, her eyes bright and alert. She did not look at him as she brushed past, kneeling so suddenly at Abigail's side that her dark green gown belled out around her legs in an aura of ash-flecked wool.

He stumbled backward, forcing himself to tear his eyes from her, to turn back to the needs of the township. Alex Somers was aiding an old man with a bad leg to a pew, supporting him from the side. He had a nasty cut above his eyebrow and appeared to have swiped the blood away with dirty hands in an effort to get this gentleman to safety, leaving bloody fingerprint smears all along the left side of his face.

"Alex," Callum said, reaching the pew just as the old man settled into a relieved recline. "What needs to be done?"

The younger Somers brother gave an ironic little laugh, his teeth bright white against his dirty face. "Fire's out, I think," he said. "I've taken yet another blow to the head. Clinic's burnt to dust, so we've got no medicine for these people. Hell if I know what should be done! I'm the useless one, remember?"

Gideon Somers approached the two of them, still somehow giving off an aura that was crisp and clean, even with spatters of blood and charcoal on his perfectly folded cravat. "The fire is out," he confirmed with enough authority that if there were still any rogue fires burning, they would surely extinguish themselves out of embarrassment. "Alex, you're covered in blood. Go get that cleaned up before that cut festers."

"Am I?" Alex replied curiously, lifting his fingers to dab at the cut and pulling them back to examine the bright red that shone on the pads of his fingers. "Well, how about that?" he marveled. "I suppose it isn't the strangest thing."

"What isn't?" Callum asked, wincing at the way the wound had opened again under prodding.

Alex Somers shrugged with a helpless, wry smile. "I hear a lot of folks bleed on their wedding night."

He wandered off, presumably in search of Dr. Garber to have his injury cleaned and stitched, leaving Callum and Gideon side by side in his wake, the latter of the two frowning in disapproval at his brother's ability to make jests at such a dire moment.

"Laughlin! Somers!" Sheldon Bywater boomed from the doors, his big frame nearly filling the doorway. "Stop standing about! We need to open the kennels and check the rest of the houses! I can see to the dogs, you two head to the eastern side of the housing block."

Gideon closed his eyes for a moment, breathing in through his nose, and then gave a curt nod, setting out to do his duty.

Callum happily followed him, back out into the anonymous chaos of loss and tragedy. Perhaps it was the only type of world that made sense to him anymore.

———

It was a strange thing, to realize all at once, well after the gentle transition to dawn, that sunlight had returned to the sky. Perhaps it was to do with the smoke-tinged fog that sat on the ground like a great thundercloud, fallen from its net. More likely it was simply the body's way of coming to terms with being pushed to its limit, choosing to cast a sort of dull veil over the experiences that ate up miserable hours so that once they were past, a man could scarcely recall them. If not for such little blessings, no one would ever survive war.

Chapter 10

Callum could scarcely account for the hours that had passed since he'd walked out of the church with Gideon Somers. He felt as charred as the buildings in the township center. Most of what remained in the thickest part of town were little more than blackened sticks and sagging foundations, still giving off a hint of steam in the bleary light of dawn. Some homes had half-survived the disaster, and now stood like grotesque memorials to what they once were. One home near the worst of the damage had its front wall completely missing, but the dinner table within still arranged with place settings, as though the family would be returning any minute to break their fast.

As they returned to the church, blinking away the shafts of sunlight that permeated their microcosm of disaster, it was like returning to Earth after a trip amongst the stars. Suddenly the eerie sounds of abandon, fear, and destruction were replaced with the low hum of human voices, the bustle of bodies overlapping with the snores of those who had found sleep, somehow, in the quiet hours that followed unspeakable horror.

He found his eyes immediately scanning the heads for a bright crown of red hair. Heloise Somers could always be counted on to stand out amongst a crowd. He wasn't sure anything would soothe his soul like seeing her, bright and beautiful and well, glowing like a beacon on the sea.

She was with that damned doctor. Even so, he felt a tightness in his chest release once his eyes had found her.

She had taken her hair down. Her green dress showed no sign of the soot and ash that smeared most everyone else, though perhaps that was only because the fabric was dark enough to disguise the stains.

She was standing poised and alert, holding a woman's arm straight and steady while the doctor smeared a fatty salve to a series of burns that marred her skin from wrist to elbow. Heloise did not flinch from the injuries, nor did she waver in touching the arm of a dirty, bleeding woman who had been born far below the station of a lady such as herself.

Such airs were not in Heloise's nature, he knew. But to see it again, on display like this, sent a pang into his heart that he had not the energy nor the lucidity to process. He had traveled to many strange and new places in the last years, and never had he met a woman—or man, for that matter!—so unconcerned with any superiority the luck of their birth had seen fit to bestow upon them.

Heloise Somers wore all of the dignity of an empress with the careless humility of a milk maid.

The injured woman was weeping silently, her face turned away from the injuries as tears streaked down the grit on her face. Heloise frowned down at her and placed a comforting hand on the other woman's neck, whispering something softly to her. Whatever she said seemed to provide the woman a modicum of comfort, for she nodded and sniffed, and wept no more.

He couldn't stand to look at her for much longer, lest his heart crumble to dust in his chest. He blinked, looking around the room for anyone else familiar, and instead falling on the only other bright flame of red hair in the room.

Alex Somers was asleep on the floor with his head in his wife's lap. He'd had the cut above his eye sewn shut with black thread hatches that contrasted quite harshly with his

Chapter 10

skin. The bride was stroking his hair with a faraway look in her eyes, her silver wedding gown covered in what looked like tiny black handprints.

"Callum," his mother called, snapping him out of his reverie.

He turned his head in time to see her hurrying over to meet him where he stood at the base of the aisle. She had tied her hair into a tight knot at the back of her head and had tied up the sides of her skirt to allow for easier movement. He was sad to see that his mother's favorite blue dress appeared to have been utterly ruined by grime and gore.

She seemed unbothered, or perhaps too tired and weary to even notice, but Callum made a mental note to buy her a new fine dress as soon as he could. Perhaps something a little more frivolous and indulgent, in that same powder blue that complemented her so.

Despite it all, Brenda Laughlin greeted her son with a broad smile and pulled him into her embrace, unconcerned with his own state of filth nor how it mingled with her own. "Oh, my boy," she crooned. "I am so proud to call you mine."

"Mother." He chuckled, giving her a firm squeeze in return. "I'm quite all right."

"Oh, I know, I know," she said breathlessly, pulling back to gaze up into his face. "But we all saw you stride in here with the Collins girl in your arms. Lady Heloise said that if you hadn't come to the rescue, the girl might very well have died! She and the babe both."

He shifted awkwardly on his feet. Heloise had gone in to save her, but he didn't know if one woman might have carried the other's dead weight successfully or for very long. The idea of Abigail having been so close to certain death was an uncomfortable one.

"Is she well, then?"

"Oh yes. Yes." His mother nodded. "Lady Heloise and the doctor both spent some time with her, getting her cleaned up and quenched. She says the babe hardly noticed all the trouble and has been kicking up a storm all morning."

The dowager viscountess approached from the direction of the pulpit, carrying a little stack of paper in her hands. "It is good to see you returned safely, Lieutenant Laughlin," she said in her broad American accent. "You and my son were the final two missing from the town census."

"Census?" Callum replied, giving a curious glance to the papers she held.

"Quite," she nodded, chestnut curls bouncing. "Reverend Halliwell keeps records in the rectory of everyone who lives in the township. We have managed to come out of this unfortunate bit of disaster fully intact. There are some injuries, but nothing life threatening and not a single casualty."

"None at all?" he marveled. "I am happy to hear it!"

"Lord Moorvale even accounted for all the horses and dogs, as well as one child's pet bunny and two rather traumatized goats," Lady Somers replied, amusement twinkling in her eyes. "We're not sure about the chickens, however. It's possible they flew into the moor to avoid the heat."

"That hound of his came in damn useful in the thick of

things," Callum told her. "She's got a very fine nose and found a couple of people we might have otherwise missed."

"I shall be sure to tell Gideon that Echo was a help," Lady Somers replied. "Perhaps he'll allow her in the dining room now."

Mrs. Laughlin scoffed. "Not likely."

Callum laughed, surprised at how good it felt, for even a small moment, to indulge in a pocket of happiness after the last hours. "Where are all these rescued animals now, might I ask?"

"At Somerton," his mother answered. "We've room in the stables and an unused kennel for the pups. The bunny, however, is here in the church, hopping around somewhere while her owner sleeps."

"Reverend Halliwell has offered up the parish house kitchen if we require it," Lady Somers said to his mother. "Though I rather think preparing a large meal at Somerton and driving it over would be more prudent."

"Yes, I'm inclined to agree. Let me gather some of the staff and we will get underway with preparing enough to feed the whole town."

Lady Somers tapped her chin, sharp and pointed just like Heloise's. "Rose is putting together a list of necessary items, building supplies, medicines, and the lot. Many people have lost all of their belongings, including their clothes, so fabric will also be an absolute necessity with how cold it is right now. If you go speak with her, she can also create a list for pantry and larder. I rather think we'll run out of food too quickly if we do not plan for it."

Mrs. Laughlin heaved a deep sigh, though Callum couldn't tell whether it was a sound of relief or trepidation. "Perhaps I will sleep on the morrow," she said with a wan little smile. "Callum, you should go get yourself seen to. That burn on your arm looks rather nasty."

Callum started, dropping his gaze to the arm his mother's eyes were affixed on. Indeed there was raw, bubbled flesh there, though from what nor when he could not possibly say. He had been so numb in the chaos of the night that he hadn't felt anything; not pain, nor fatigue, nor fear. Even now, as he became aware of his body again, his stomach rumbled loudly.

Mrs. Laughlin narrowed her eyes, as though her son had released the tell-tale grumble of hunger on purpose to hasten her in her task, but Lady Somers only laughed.

"Come along, young man," the dowager said, taking his unburnt arm in her cool, manicured hand. "Let's get you settled."

11

Heloise lifted her arms over her head, indulging in a long, languorous stretch in this brief moment of rest. She had seen to so many people in the last few hours that she had lost count of them. Her mother had stopped by as she worked, questioning each of the injured for their names, families, and the state of their home as last they had seen it, while Reverend Halliwell was doing the same along the walls where people were camping for the night.

The church's position at the rear of town had been planned as a matter of convenience, for it was where the cemetery had been for hundreds of years and could continue to expand for a couple hundred more. Because it was so far from every other building, it had been the safest place in the township last night, far removed from any flames that might leap across a roof shingle or from one window to the next.

She had unwrapped the ribbon from her hair some time ago, as the pressure from it had begun to make her head hurt. She had braided her long, red tresses down her back in a loose plait and secured the end with the long length of green ribbon, as not to lose it, and continued her work with one less irritation distracting her from her charges.

Once she had been certain that Abigail Collins and her unborn child were safe and well, everything else had felt so easy. Even so, she was still fighting the urge to go disturb the sleeping Abigail and inspect her one more time, just to be certain.

She would never forget the sight of Callum Laughlin bursting out of that cottage with Abigail in his arms, his face stony and determined, his tall and broad frame supporting her as she lolled right on the edge of life and death. If he had been half so spectacular during the war, it was no wonder he'd earned an officer's title and a medal to boot. It was no wonder at all.

Abigail had come to in stages, her lucidity sharpening a little more each time. Heloise had carefully sponged the dust and dirt from her arms, legs, neck, and face. She'd combed her hair as gently as she could, ensuring that none had been charred nor any burns had come to her scalp as she lay on the floor.

She wondered what was left of the little Collins cottage. Would they ever be able to dispel the smell of smoke after last night? She thought perhaps not. It seemed impossible that the township would ever smell of anything but fire again.

"Heloise, darling," her mother's voice sang in that tone that always preceded a request of some sort.

Hel turned, gritting her teeth tightly to avoid visibly startling at the sight of Callum Laughlin on her mother's arm.

He looked an absolute fright, as though he'd spent the last hour rolling about in a pile of coal dust. His fine shirt and trousers were absolutely ruined, with several small holes burnt into the shirt and streaks of filth along his trousers. His shirtsleeves were rolled up, revealing the fine musculature of his forearms, one of which looked rather red and blistered.

"The young lieutenant has sustained a burn injury." Ruthie Somers pouted, patting his uninjured arm. "Might you see to his wounds and assist him in washing up? I'm sure he'll wish to return to the manor as soon as possible and get some sleep."

"Of course, Mother," Heloise demurred, turning her eyes cooly to Callum, who shuffled forward awkwardly and stood on the riser next to her, where her medical kit was still spread out with an assortment of creams and potions that the doctor had provided. She held her mother's eye with an expressionless stare until Ruthie finally gave a sigh of defeat and turned on her heel, returning to her business with the reverend.

Dr. Garber was with Rose, compiling a list of things to be retrieved from York at the soonest possibility. It was dumb luck that he'd had his medical bag in the carriage at Somerton last night, rather than having left it in the clinic as usual. If he had, they would have lost absolutely everything to the blaze.

She did not often wish for Richard to hover near her the way he was prone to doing, but just now it would have been a welcome intervention.

"Your mother looks just the same," Callum said politely, his hands clasped awkwardly in front of him. "I can't remember when I saw her last, but I recognized her immediately."

"She has always been lovely," Heloise agreed, keeping a neutrality to her tone as she held her hand out for his arm. "Though she certainly is not identical to the woman who departed Yorkshire some fifteen years ago. Please sit."

He cleared his throat, easing down onto the riser with the type of uncertain awkwardness she hadn't seen him display since before she'd been sent to boarding school. She noted, with some amusement, that the arm he had injured was the same one he'd been wearing in a sling the day she'd been shipped off. He'd broken it assisting her with a silly prank to terrorize one of her governesses, and instead had spooked her horse, which had in turn given him a swift and brutal kick in said arm.

"Come on, then," she tutted, holding out her hands for his arm. "Let's have a look."

"Oh, of course. Apologies." He stuck out his wrist, averting his eyes from her inspection.

She forced herself to reach out and grip his wrist, his bare skin touching hers by her own volition for the first time in a very long time. She kept a mask of placidity on as she pulled his heavy, muscled arm into her lap and turned his wrist upward to make inspecting the burns easier.

If she could see beneath the grime on his face, she rather suspected that he would be blushing, which was of course ridiculous for a man who was saving people from burning buildings not two hours prior.

She waited, allowing the warmth of connected skin to settle

Chapter 11

into normalcy, and took the opportunity to study his face while his eyes were directed elsewhere. He was still beautiful, she thought, even at his most weary, and still so strong, as evidenced by the weight of muscle in her hands.

She followed the path of his gaze to her mother, who was giggling at something the reverend had said, while he blushed and chuckled along with her.

"She started flirting with the reverend during the party we threw this autumn," Heloise said, her voice cutting through the moment with an effective clap of reality. She dropped her attention back onto his injured arm, finding it easier to talk of family gossip than to confront the fact that the two of them were in such close quarters. "We can't make sense of it."

"What do you mean?" Callum turned to face her, his tone steady but his movements those of a man desperate for any sort of conversation.

"Mother has always been two things, very beautiful and very calculating. What she could possibly think to achieve by encouraging the flirtations of a country vicar with a paunch and white hair is beyond us."

"I see," he replied, in a voice that made it apparent he did not.

She gave a little smile, reaching down for a burn salve to apply to his arm. The sensation of her fingers plunging into the icy paste was strangely grounding opposite everything else she was feeling.

There was almost a sort of charm in his innocence, she thought. He sincerely believed that a woman born to fortune like Ruthie Cunningham Somers could truly entertain the flirtations of such a man. Even without her mother's shrewd approach to her life's choices, the scenario was obviously untenable to anyone with any sense of the harsh rules of the world they lived in.

Gideon had said some weeks ago, during a game of hazard after dinner, that perhaps their mother simply enjoyed the reverend's company and desired the innocent connection of friendship. This had resulted in such an exchange of skeptical expressions between Alex and Hel that Gideon had actually been cowed into silence for once.

She sucked in a little breath as she applied the salve to the raw and blistered path of his burns. Heloise was not a squeamish woman, and had seen far worse by way of injury and gore, but for some reason, seeing him marred so made her stomach roil. It made tears want to well up in her eyes. It was even worse than the electric warmth of holding his undamaged wrist just moments before.

"How did you come by this injury?" she asked, turning to reach for more ointment. She twisted her entire body in an effort to avoid his eye as his head snapped around in surprise. She forced the tone of her voice into a brusqueness of professional necessity, taking a little too much time to collect the cream onto her fingers, and added, "I can better treat a wound if I know how and when it was sustained."

He was quiet for a moment, those black eyes burning into her until she raised her own eyes to meet them, her heart slamming itself insistently against her ribs.

"I don't remember," he said quietly, holding her gaze with a soft, almost peaceful depth to his eyes. "I didn't even know

I'd burnt it until my mother pointed it out just a few moments ago. I suppose I likely bumped into a plank of wood or some such that was still very hot."

Heloise frowned, looking down again at the raw and blistered skin, gently swirling the ointment around to encourage it to absorb. "I suppose it might be the way women are said to forget the true pain of childbirth once it is over, so that they are not plagued with the memory of such pain."

"I think it is more likely that I was lost in the task set out for me and nothing else could puncture that frame of mind," he replied, dropping his gaze to watch her fingers on his skin. "It does not hurt, really, and I have been burned before."

Heloise bit her tongue, wishing against hope that she could avoid taking the bait of a statement like that. If she had heeded her finishing school education half so well as her new sister-in-law, she could easily have replied with some cutting witticism that would have prevented him from trying such tactics again.

Alas, she had never been a very good student.

"Hurt in the war, you mean?" she asked, shushing the part of her mind that immediately cursed her weakness of spirit.

"A few times," he agreed, a strange little smile playing on his lips. "But I was more referring to the time this particular arm was snapped in two by a particularly well-placed kick from Boudicea."

Heloise flushed, a begrudging amusement sending a curve into the corners of her lips. "And you shall heal just as completely this time, I should think."

"Last time, I was rewarded for my efforts with a kiss," he reminded her, his tone of voice still even and quiet, as though he were simply recounting an innocent story from the past. "It hastened my recovery."

Heloise froze, her fingers lying on his arm, stopped from performing a task that had already been complete for some time. She lifted her head to meet his eye again, though every time she did it, she knew it was a mistake.

"I was fifteen," she said softly. "It was a very long time ago."

"It was," he agreed. He drew his arm slightly back, far enough that when he flipped his hand over, Heloise's palm landed in his own, dwarfed by the large, calloused presence of the proof that he had been born to a far different lot in life than she.

She knew she ought to snatch her hand back, gather her skirts, and march away. It would be grievous error to encourage him in any small way, no matter how weary they were nor how out of character one might behave in such an unusual moment. She knew what she ought to do, and did nothing anyway, allowing him to hold her hand in his for a stolen moment of silence, while he gazed down upon their connecting flesh with an expression like a man observing the finest art.

"Heloise," Gideon's voice rang out, causing both of them to snap their hands back into their own laps.

She stood, brushing imaginary debris from her skirt as her brother approached. "Yes?"

Gideon drew up to a level with her and gave a nod of acknowledgement down to where Callum still sat on the

Chapter 11

riser. "Rose and I are headed into York in a few hours, while Gloriana and Alex have opted to cancel their tour of the Continent to stay on and assist. The Blakelys have offered to remain as well, so I am sending them to Leeds. Supplies must be collected quickly and from places most like to have them. I need you to take charge of the estate in my absence and direct Alex and Gloriana to whatever tasks need to be undertaken."

"Me?" she repeated, blinking at him in astonishment. "In charge of the estate?"

"Well, of course," he replied easily. "Can you imagine Alex in charge of the place?"

"No," she admitted with a little frown. "What about Mother?"

Gideon did not answer, instead leveling her with a flat stare that made his feelings on the matter clear enough. Once she'd nodded in understanding, he continued, "You will need to find a way to keep everyone housed, warm, and fed while we seek out aid and materials to rebuild. Sheldon is going to make a run to Moorvale when there is time to see about temporary accommodations and perhaps loaned supplies. Reverend Halliwell has said that people may make camp here in the church for as long as necessary, but we all know that is not a solution that will hold out until the spring."

"It won't," she agreed, her mind beginning to whir with the routes she might take to a solution.

"Lieutenant Laughlin," Gideon continued, stopping Callum before he could slip away. "If you could remain as well and aid my sister in this endeavor, we would be much obliged. I understand that this type of disaster management was something you encountered at war, and as such, you might help us streamline the process."

"Of course," Callum replied, his body going rigid and alert, as though he were responding to a commanding officer. "Anything I can do to help. I am at your disposal."

"Perfect." Gideon sighed, relief evident on his face. "The two of you working together should get this place back on its feet in short order."

Heloise did not respond. It was one of the few moments in her life that she found herself entirely speechless.

She wasn't ready to return to Somerton. She couldn't. Not just yet.

She stood sentry over the inner sanctum of the church as bowls of porridge and steaming cups of tea were circulated to people wrapped in blankets, to be eaten in the pews or on the floor, with no division between the two on account of nobility or status. Heloise found she had no appetite, nor did she feel prepared to return home, bathe, and fall into the reassuring oblivion of dead sleep.

She was being left the run of the manor, and with it the entire township. It was enough to make her light-headed. Where could she even begin at this time of year, with all of the others spread out to various waypoints throughout the north? She knew she could not herself leave Somerton in search of aid, not with one of her charges so close to giving birth, and in truth there was very little that had ever tempted her away from Yorkshire, and never for very long besides.

It was only that she was being left here with *him*. And not in some casual capacity in the manor house where she might simply make herself scarce until his eventual departure. No, she was actually going to need Callum in the coming days to assist in managing the consequences of the fire.

She felt an itch to survey exactly what damage the blaze had wrought, even if the embers were still glowing and warm on the ground. More than one person had relayed to her that the clinic was forfeit, but if she could salvage even a few things from the rubble, it could make all the difference.

Slowly and silently, so as to not attract the attention of anyone who might stop her, she lifted her cloak from its hook near the door and slipped out of the church through a crack in the great entry doors. She stepped into the blinding whiteness of mid-morning without so much as a squint of discomfort at the sudden assault of light. The snow was falling in lazy gusts, making slow work of covering up the charred skeleton of the town with a redemption of white frost, but all the same, the ground was frosty enough to throw the meager sunlight directly back into the world with a strength only found in the winter.

She shivered, throwing the hood up over her unkempt braid and tucking the stray red curls that framed her face beneath it. Boudicea was still tethered to the tree outside of the church and appeared to be sleeping, as though the world around her were not a terrifying and unfamiliar thing. Sweet Boudicea was always so constant, so reassuring. Heloise did not know what she would do without her, but did not want to interrupt the one soul who had found peace on this weary morn.

The ground was slick and slippery with brittle layers of ice, formed from the snow that had melted under the heat of the chaos, then rapidly refrozen in the frigid air. It would make walking through the town treacherous for many people, particularly the elderly and the young. She made a mental note to have it broken up or salted at the first opportunity, wondering where Mrs. Laughlin kept an inventory of what they had available in the pantry for such a task.

The smell was not so bad as it had been, she thought. Or perhaps she had simply grown accustomed to it. She only tasted a tinge of smoke on the cold, arid breaths that filled her lungs.

The inn appeared to be minimally impacted. Perhaps she could convince the innkeeper to open up his rooms at no charge for some of the displaced townspeople. If he demanded compensation, surely she could arrange for something reasonable to be paid from the Somerton coffers. After all, part of the duty of a viscount was to oversee the welfare of his county, was it not? And for a short time, she was going to be viscount.

She must ask Gideon for the accounts before he was off to York. The particularities of the running of Somerton had never been much more than a vagary to her, but she did know how to balance a ledger thanks to her hard-fought education at Mrs. Arlington's School for Young Ladies.

Perhaps, despite the difficulties they would have rebuilding, it had been a small blessing that this fire had happened in the winter, when there were no crops nearby to be

Chapter 11

destroyed. They had far less to manage in replacing housing and supplies than they would have in losing an entire season's harvest and all of the incidental benefits that derived from the agricultural industry around Somerton.

She glanced down at the footprints she was making on the cobbled path. Each step dented in the fresh powder of snow, with a layer of soot in the edges and a glassy reflection of ice at the center. It was like the trunk of a tree, split open with its rings visible to anyone who cared to track the years that had passed from one experience to the next, laying bare all the stages of its life. This had been a very long night.

She drew herself up to a complete, abrupt stop at the sight of the clinic. In truth, she had expected worse. The way it had been described to her, right at the center of the fire's origin, she had thought nothing would remain but a blackened rectangle where the building once stood, or perhaps, if they were lucky, a few beams to indicate that once there had been the sturdy safety of a fully realized structure.

Instead, it looked rather like a boiled egg that had been scooped out with a spoon. The exterior's geometric shape had softened beyond recognition, collapsing upon itself in a nebulous melding of beams and walls rather than a constructed building. Remains of furniture spilled out onto the snow like a broken yolk, while strips of wallpaper and the skeleton of shelving clung to the two and a half walls that still stood. The staircase was visible, apparently intact, leading up to the loft where dried herbs and compounds were kept, though from the ground, she could not gauge what might have survived at the higher level.

Her heart was racing in her chest, emotion thick in her throat. She felt for a moment completely unable to move.

Somehow what remained was so much more than she had expected while also being so much worse than she had prepared herself for. It hurt seeing the place she'd come to think of as her own, the thing she'd watched being built, where she'd learned to practice midwifery on her own in ruins, brought so very, very low. The indignity of it, the desecration of this place, hit her square in the chest, as though a very dear friend had died.

She wondered if perhaps it would have hurt less if there was nothing left, rather than seeing the clinic like this. Mutilated.

She bit down on her tongue to force herself out of her trance, gripping her cloak in her fists. There was nothing to be done now but to see what she could salvage and to work toward rebuilding. She stepped over the doorless threshold, forcing herself to inhale the scent of charred cedar wood, to acknowledge the truth of what was around her. The window frames were all empty, the glass having long since exploded from the pressure of the heat, and much of the debris on the floor appeared to be from the four cots that were arranged on the ground level.

She approached the base of the staircase, squinting up at the path to the second level. If she walked slowly and tested each step before putting her full weight upon it, surely she could reach the top without issue. It was doomed to collapse eventually, and surely it would be a horrible waste not to recover whatever might remain up there.

She put one booted foot forward, gripping her hand against the exposed and blackened bricks, and leaned forward. The pained creaking was ominous, but the stair held, even when she set her full weight upon it. The relief she felt that even

Chapter 11

this one step may still retain its strength was enough to wrench a strangled sob from her throat. She squeezed her eyes together, willing away the hot tears that sprang to the corners of her eyes, inhaled deeply, and set another foot forward.

She let out a yelp of surprise, not from the floor giving way but from a strong set of arms that appeared from the ether, wrapping around her waist and lifting her full off her feet, toes dangling. She squirmed, her breath caught in her throat, and as soon as her boots touched the charred ground, she spun around with fury in her eyes to confront her assailant.

Callum Laughlin looked exasperated, his dark eyes narrowed on Heloise's face. Before she could demand an explanation, he was already speaking, his voice a hiss of frustration. "What the hell are you doing?" he snapped. "Do you want to fall to your death?"

"It's none of your concern!" she gasped, indignity flooding her every limb. "How dare you handle me so!"

He scoffed, shaking his head in disbelief. "I've handled you quite a bit more thoroughly than that, Heloise. Let's not pretend otherwise. If you had fallen through that staircase, you could have been seriously injured, and no one would have known. You could've broken a leg and frozen to death, all by yourself out here."

"Obviously not," she retorted, pushing her hood back in frustration, her cheeks burning. "Since you were following me for some ridiculous reason!"

"It is extremely obvious when you are up to something," he said, crossing his arms over his broad chest. "You're lucky it was me that spotted you and not one of your brothers."

She huffed, dropping her hands on her hips to prevent herself from attempting to strangle him. "My brothers respect me enough to allow me to make my own choices!"

He didn't respond, though the flat line of his mouth spoke volumes regarding his belief of that statement. After a beat of tense silence, he sighed, dropping his arms to his sides, and glanced up at the staircase he had plucked her from. "What do you need up there?"

"Whatever has survived," she replied. "Anything at all that can be recovered would make a world of difference."

He inhaled deeply, setting his jaw, and glanced around until his eyes landed on a particularly solid beam of wood, just thin enough to be held in his hand. He crossed the room, coming close enough to her that she felt a stirring of air, and retrieved it, then gestured to the staircase.

"I will go first," he said, holding out the stick. "My weight will test each stair. Then press on it with this before you attempt to stand on it yourself. Understand?"

She snatched the wood from him, the uneven grain biting into the soft flesh of her palms. "Fine. Just go!"

His eyes lingered on her a moment, glittering against the slats of sunlight that invaded the destroyed room. It was clear he had many thoughts that he'd like to voice in that moment, but none of them came forward. Instead he turned on his heel and approached the staircase, beginning an ascent that Heloise thought was damn near identical to the one she had been attempting.

Chapter 11

She followed behind him, faithfully testing each step with the wooden stick before putting her weight upon it. Only one stair was unsafe, its foundation splitting with a crack that made her jump something fierce as Callum's boot went through it. His only reaction was a click of irritation and a wider step onto the next level, with barely a pause to indicate that he might have easily hurt himself if he'd gone too quickly.

At the top, a gap had formed between the staircase and the loft platform that made up the floor of the upper level. Callum's wide stride made easy work of it. After a few well-placed stomps around the area of the loft floor, he seemed satisfied with its integrity, and he turned, holding out his arms to Heloise to assist her across.

As much as she wished she could reject the gesture and simply vault herself across, she knew that she ought not to risk it. She gripped his forearms, her fingers as light as possible against the bandages on his left arm as his hands came around her waist. She held her breath against the lurch of emotion in her throat as he swept her from the top stair and set her safely down on the loft floor.

They looked at one another for a moment, each one still holding on to the other. Heloise dropped her arms first, muttering a thanks as she stepped away from his grip, his calloused fingers sliding away from her hips and down to the sides of his body.

She forced herself to swallow, turning her back on him and blinking rapidly in an effort to quiet the emotions roiling about within her. How was she going to survive having him so close again? He had been vexing enough when it was only his shade at her side.

Focusing on the room didn't do much to calm her. Her careful catalogue of useful herbs and compounds was a demolished wreck. The bottles and jars lined up so lovingly upon the shelving on the walls had collapsed, leaving nothing but charred stems and shattered glass. Months of work gone, as though it had never existed at all.

A few glimmers of silver beneath the wicked shards of broken containers perhaps hinted at the possibility of a few salvageable tools, though she wasn't sure how much use they'd ever be again, spoiled and coated in soot and glass.

For the first time in a long time, she felt utterly powerless. Defeated. She stood as listless and useless as a child, looking upon the remains of the life she had built, of the love she'd chosen after he had left her all alone, this thing she'd built from the ruins of despair after her dreams had been dashed. Tears stung at her eyes, which she could not seem to tear away from the remains of her last hopes for the clinic.

What legacy would she have for her daughter now? What comfort would she have in the night, alone forevermore in her cold bed? Even if there had been one solitary pinch of her medicines, one sprig of her herbs, but no ... It was all gone. This thing she'd built and nurtured and grown had been just as fragile as anything else she'd ever believed in, anything else she'd ever taken pride in or trusted. She wanted to crumble to the same ash that coated the ground outside.

"Heloise," Callum said, his voice softer than before, and closer than she realized. He set a hand upon her shoulder, warm and solid and whole, perhaps the only thing on this frozen earth that could penetrate the chill in her skin. "It will be all right."

Chapter 11

She let the air from her lungs, her eyes squeezing shut and releasing hot streaks of misery down the sides of her face. She should have gone home, she thought. She should have just gone to sleep. It would have been better not to know. How would she ever find oblivion now? How would she ever breathe again?

"Hel ..." he murmured, that damned voice still so deep and delicious, so familiar and tempting.

How was she meant to bear it? All of it. How could the universe throw so much at one woman and expect her to remain upright?

An indignant anger bubbled in her chest at the injustice of it all, at the cruelty of it. Sadness fizzled away under the heat of her rage, warming her against the cold, suffocating the misery in her heart in favor of red-hot indignation.

"Shut up," she whispered, spinning on her heel to face him. "Just ... please, Callum."

She gripped his tattered shirt in her hands, pulling her body up against his. She held her lips just a whisper from his own, turning her green eyes up to meet his black ones. She could feel his heart thundering in his chest, could feel the way his breath hitched at this sudden closeness. His body was so gloriously warm, radiating a heady aura of something that sent glorious, thawing heat into her blood.

"Heloise," he choked.

She lifted herself up onto her toes, pushing her mouth against his, desperate for the bliss of being overtaken by anything but the horror that had fallen upon them in the last several hours. She knew it was wrong. She knew it was a mistake. Perhaps that's why it was so effective. "Please," she said again, against his lips. "I need you."

He ceased to hesitate in returning her kiss, releasing a soft, helpless groan against her lips as one big hand came around her waist and the other dug itself into her braided hair, spilling tresses from the messy plait to fall around her face. He kissed her ravenously, like he had wanted to do nothing else for all his life.

The sensation of it tore through Heloise like a flame, demolishing all the nagging thoughts and distressed emotions that wished to freeze her blood and render her helpless. In his arms, there was nothing else but the relief of coming home again and the surge of pure desire that can only be born of long-suffered neglect.

Her fingertips traveled down his chest, over the taut muscle of his stomach, to the waistband of his trousers. She did not care for seductions nor propriety. She wanted all of him right now, immediately. She wanted what she had been so long denied.

He made a sound as though he might protest, perhaps out of concern that they would be seen, half-sheltered as they were in a building that had partially collapsed. Perhaps this wasn't how he envisioned finding his way back into her arms. Callum always had been wistful and romantic, and there simply wasn't room for such sentiment nor gentleness in a world that could fall apart so completely so quickly.

He couldn't hide how much he wanted her, not straining as he was against the brush of her fingers as she unlaced his trousers. Touching him even in this sparing way made his body glow with heat against her own, his hold on her becoming more urgent, more fierce.

She loved feeling so very vulnerable in this way. Callum's strength and size were a reminder to her how truly fragile she was, despite the power she felt she wielded in this stolen moment.

She urged him to follow her to the charred floorboards, her skirts and cloak pooling around their legs as they fell to a kneeling embrace. For all his superiority of size and strength, she was the one who held the control. He went happily onto his back, her hair falling in a ruby waterfall around them.

All would be well if only the kissing could continue, if only their connection would not be severed.

The smell of him was enough to bring tears rising up in her throat again. Somehow through the layers of ash, he was still Callum Laughlin; he was still that boy she had loved year after year, season after season. Still the one with whom she'd shared the careless and giddy games of childhood and the misdirected awkwardness following that first blush of attraction. They had grown together, become who they were together. It was no wonder it had all come to its peak during that storm-riddled summer when she was nineteen.

Despite it all. Despite knowing it would never be perfect again, they both knew they had been shaped for one another. They both knew it could never be the same with anyone else.

The charred floorboards were rough against her knees, split and splintered and blackened as they were. It did not matter. She left the luxury of touching him only to work her own skirts higher, to free her tangled thighs from the prison of many layers of winter warmth. She wished they could be skin to skin, but if she stopped to think about how to make that possible, the spell would break, and it would be too late.

"Hel, it's too cold," he breathed, his words a cloud of steam in the recess between them. No matter his warnings, he couldn't seem to stop his big hands tracing down the column of her throat, sliding over her breasts and down to grip her waist. Both of them were trapped in a dance of instinct where logical concerns had no charter whatsoever.

"I'll keep you warm," she assured him in a throaty whisper, lifting her hips only long enough to spread her skirt and cloak out around the two of them, with only one hand still hidden beneath to guide him into her.

There was no need for anything else. She had been slick and ready for him from the moment he'd returned her kiss. Their joining felt as inevitable as breathing, and for all that it was familiar, the absolute rightness of it, the quick gasp of recognition at the way they fit one another was enough to cloud her mind past the ability to think of anything at all.

She could swear she smelled the hayloft, that for a solitary, magical moment they were transported back through time, to that heady summer of discovery and passion. He felt so familiar to her, so perfectly right. She gripped her hands against his chest as she rode him, meeting the thrusts of his own hips. She dipped herself forward to catch his mouth with her own as they pushed one another into raw, primal oblivion.

Her eyes closed against the swirls of ash and snow, against the bleak brightness of the morning, and instead she

Chapter 11

tumbled through time, curled on his bed by lantern light with the moon streaming in from the slats above, balmy wind stirring their hair as he read to her about the great leaders of the ancient world. Her thighs clenched against his hips and she felt the crackle of gathering clouds, the wind heavy and sharp as they galloped across an endless green moor in search of hidden caves and secret kisses. She could taste the laughter on their lips as he swept her into shadowed corners of Somerton, stealing embraces where he could, until the moon was high again and she might sneak out to be with him yet again.

She didn't know when the tears started to flow down her cheeks again. It didn't matter because she couldn't feel them. She could only feel this and the undeniable demands of her body, driving her to grasp Callum and the abyss of this perfect familiarity. She was almost disappointed when she felt the first shudder of climax thrumming through her, the warning peal before the heavy crash of ultimate pleasure. She felt him catch her, heard his breath, hot and steady as he drove himself upward in quick, precise thrusts.

He must have found his own pleasure while she was still in the throes of her own, for by the time she caught her breath again and the haze had begun to clear, he was already slack beneath her, his eyes closed and his lips parted. His muscled chest rose and fell, his heart beating steadily beneath the warmth of his flesh. She allowed herself to really, truly look at him, to revisit the beautiful lines of his face, the shape of his mouth, the way his hair stubbornly set in a wave just above his brow.

Did he look older? Was he hardened by battle? In this moment, she couldn't say he was. He was the man who had shared her bed and haunted her dreams all those years ago, and no other.

She couldn't resist reaching forward to stroke his face, to twine her fingers through those snow-kissed strands of hair. She knew it was only a matter of time before the panic must inevitably find her, before she was on her feet and fleeing from him again, but just now, in the glow of satisfaction that followed an unexpected blossom of beauty amidst utter ruin, she couldn't bring herself to hasten its arrival.

He had come home again. He had lived. He was whole. He still loved her.

Another time she might have wept for the relief of it, but all of her tears had been spent.

Instead, she spread her cloak out around the both of them and leaned forward, resting her head into the recess of his shoulder, a place that seemed to have been shaped exactly for the curve of her cheek. She closed her eyes as his arms came up around her, and together they breathed in silence, allowing comfort to simply exist, if only for a moment.

12

They hadn't spoken much, afterward.

Callum supposed it was for the best. Both of them were so physically exhausted and so emotionally raw that nothing coherent could have come from heavy conversation that morning anyhow. Still, for a brief moment, she had given him her trust again. For a single moment, she had given him herself.

That said more than any words possibly could, didn't it?

They'd ridden Boudicea together back to Somerton. Heloise had nestled herself into the curve of his chest, allowing him control of her mare for the journey. Again, that level of trust spoke volumes. The smell of her hair and the warmth of her little body was almost intoxicating enough to drive him back to the place he'd found on the floor of that burnt-out clinic. He knew better, though. He knew that in that moment, what she needed was steadiness and comfort, not passion. Not lust. Certainly not demands.

He held her close and assisted her down when they reached

the manor, passing her over to the fretting arms of a maid who ushered her up to her old rooms, murmuring reassurances in her ear. He'd led her mare into the stall he knew belonged to her, and had swallowed an unexpected lump that rose in his throat when Boudicea nudged him with a nicker of recognition, as though to say, "I'm glad you're home too, stable boy."

He made his way into the manor, coming only into the foyer before realizing he had no idea where to go. He did not know where his things had been taken, nor if any of the beds in the servants' quarters were open for a weary body. He was stuck in place, with nothing to do but gaze up at the painting of nineteen-year-old Heloise Somers that sat above the entry to Somerton. The summer it had been painted was the last of the time they had spent together, and it had captured her fire most beautifully. She sat, stroking Nero as a kitten, a mischievous sparkle in her bottle-green eyes and a knowing smirk hovering near the corner of her lips. She was young and vibrant in a gown of brilliant turquoise. Even in this state, well past fatigue, he still found himself in awe of her.

"Sir?" a voice echoed from the halls. "Lieutenant?"

Callum turned, blinking against his fatigue, to see a familiar face making his way toward him.

"Albert!" He felt the ghost of a welcoming smile finding its way onto his mouth. This footman had been the epitome of masculinity to him as a lad, an impressive and debonair fellow that always left the scullery maids sighing after him. "I didn't see you earlier. You look well!"

"Thank you, Lieutenant," Albert replied with cool polite-

Chapter 12

ness. He shifted his weight, a distinct look of uncertainty passing over his features. After a moment's silence, he added, awkwardly, "It is good to have you safely returned."

Callum's smile slipped from his lips as quickly as it had appeared. For just a second, he had forgotten that everything was different now.

"I don't suppose you might show me to where I'm sleeping?" Callum said, too weary to insist on familiarity. "Perhaps I might have a bath drawn as well?"

Far from taking offense, Albert looked relieved, as though Callum assuming the role of a gentleman was far easier for him to stomach than any nebulous outlier who hovered between classes. He gave a crisp nod and held his arm out in the direction of the staircase, indicating that Callum's accommodations would be abovestairs, in one of the lush guest rooms on the second floor.

The room itself was far more opulent than any space Callum had ever occupied. Its sheer size was larger than some of the houses he had imagined himself owning, in the more optimistic days of his youth. In the center of the room, quilted and piled with pillows, was a massive four-poster bed that he could swear was singing to him, calling him into its embrace.

"I shall have the bath water brought presently," Albert informed him, his posture stiff and respectful. "We've already got several pots heated, in anticipation of those who are returning from the township. Might I bring you a spot of food or anything else, Lieutenant?"

Callum shook his head, his eyes falling on the array of materials already laid out for him—combs and a razor on a leather strip, soaps and towels and even a pair of bedroom slippers. He had no appetite to speak of and wasn't sure he would have been able to taste much over his fatigue anyhow. "I think I've more than enough here, thank you."

Albert gave a curt nod, turning on his heel to see to his business. It wasn't until his hand was already turning the knob on the door that he hesitated, pausing in his movement without turning back.

"It is truly good to have you home, Callum," he said quietly. "We were all very worried."

"It is good to be home," Callum replied, a smile spreading unbidden to his lips as the other man exited the room in search of the promised bathwater. Those simple words had put a warmth into his bones that even the most luxurious bath could never have matched.

He sat on a bench at the foot of the bed, kicking off his shoes with a relieved sigh, and leaned back against the footboard. He realized that it was true, despite all the missteps he'd made, despite the fire and the heartbreak and the state of the bridge he must mend to find his way fully back to Heloise. He was home, and glad of it, no matter which bedroom they stuffed him in.

It was a thought that stayed with him, comforting as a warm fleece and light as the bubbles of soap that rose from the bathtub. It was a feeling that kept a curve on his lips as he dried and dressed and crawled into that obscenely big bed. It was the hope that took him swiftly to sleep, filled with optimism for what the morrow might bring.

Chapter 12

There was no gentle launch into the process of rebuilding the township.

The church had emptied by about half in the day following the fire, with those who were able returning to their homes. Those who remained were gifted whatever small offerings their neighbors could spare in the way of bedding, clothing, and food. Many of the little ones also volunteered their toys to their friends whose own things had been lost to the flames.

It was surprising how quickly those in charge of the restoration efforts fell into a pattern. Callum would never say so out loud, but he found the people of Somerton to be rather more efficient than the Royal Arms ever had been, especially for the task of building rather than destruction.

The girl Alex Somers had married, the pretty little blonde he'd imagined delicately flitting through balls and hosting tea parties, was in actuality a shrewd and exacting accountant, whose keeping of the expense ledgers and lending receipts left more than one full-grown man walking away with an armful of supplies borrowed from the manor house, wide-eyed and muttering to himself.

The local children seemed to have a fixation on her, which she bore with brief smiles and endless little quests to keep them out of the way while she worked, much to her husband's amusement.

"You know," Alex had chuckled to Callum as they'd hauled lumber through the churchyard, "I can't tell if the way she herds those children means she'd make a wonderful mother or a horrid one."

"They think she is a princess," Callum had told him, having overheard many breathless conversations to that nature from the children he'd been dodging in his work.

"Mm." Alex had sighed fondly. "And she's not one to correct them either."

As to Heloise, she had been primarily in the township itself, taking stock of the damage and what was salvageable in the way of wood and stone from the damaged buildings. She had met his eye more than once, a sphinx-like mystery of a smile playing about her lips, and then turned back to her tasks before he had much time at all to attempt to decipher what she might have meant by it.

He was reasonably certain that she wasn't deliberately avoiding him anymore, however. The work itself had consumed all of them in its intensity, and left them all so depleted by the end that there was nothing to do but trudge home and fall back into bed until it was time to begin again.

Perhaps it had taken a night for Callum's scent to find the room in which he was staying, but every night since the first, he had arrived back at Somerton to find Nero curled into his blankets, awaiting the additional warmth of his chosen human bedfellow. Callum found that even if Nero had chosen the exact center of the bed, he preferred to adjust his body around the cat rather than attempt to move him. He told himself it was out of a desire to avoid being scratched, but deep down, he knew he simply did not wish to disturb such endearing slumber.

His own mother had been much at Somerton during this time, continuing to prepare porridge in the morning and soup for the evening, with cold meats and cheeses sent in between. This food fed everyone alike and was essential to keep the laborers and survivors going day by day. He knew she would be just as hard worn as the rest of them, even if she was not in the thick of it, and likely distressed to be overseeing such paltry offerings day after day. Still, it was the best way to extend the rations of food they had available, and no one had uttered a single word of complaint, only gratitude.

The dowager viscountess and the reverend worked closely together to manage the church's temporary guests, attempting to keep the injured ones fed and entertained as the rest worked around them. The doctor made so many rounds in the span of each day that he had begun to take on a sallow appearance, as though he might keel over himself soon, which would put them all in a fine lurch.

It was well when the dowager instructed him to take a day to rest in the tone of an American businesswoman who would broker no argument. Callum felt somewhat guilty resenting the man for his open and bold interest in Heloise when he was so clearly run down, though it was not enough to instill him with any friendly impulses.

The first of the dispersed aid to return was Sheldon Bywater, whose manor was only a day's ride away at a gallop. He came with two carriages, filled to the brim with all manner of necessities and two young men from amongst Graham the driver's brood to assist with the work. It was the youngest son, the stable boy Robbie, who jumped first from the carriage, with a parcel in his arms and a look of determined ferocity on his face, off to some mysterious destination with his supplies.

Sheldon ... that is, Lord Moorvale, for all his persistent joviality, was a seasoned military officer and a marquis besides. He knew when and how to bark orders which would be followed quickly and effectively. Still, authority did not put a damper on his general amicability, though somehow he was able to balance the two without ever compromising an air of necessity to his commands. Perhaps it was just the sheer size and presence of the man that did it, though Callum thought that even a dwarf of a man with Moorvale's countenance might be just as effective. Something about his general *joie de vivre* was unarguably contagious.

Soon, a startling number of township residents were wrapped in Moorvale tartan, staving off the cold like proper Scots in a weave of blue and gold, which seemed to put Sheldon himself into an even better mood than usual, giving him an air of energy as he bustled around, directing this and that into its designated place. Only a few hours after his arrival, they had stockpiles of coal, lumber, stone, and fabric for Heloise to use as she saw fit.

The first time Heloise spoke to him, some days into the project, was unfortunately in the context of addressing a group of the most able physical laborers and the Somerton household members involved in the disaster management.

"Tomorrow, we will begin the process of pulling down the ruined buildings," she informed them, upright and confident as any lord of the Realm. "We've three experienced carpenters here to guide us in the process, but I think to be safe, we ought to evacuate the surrounding buildings while we work. If, by the end, we have intact foundations upon which we might feasibly begin rebuilding, we may make better time in restoring the township to its original state than we initially believed. All in all, it has been a very encouraging week, and I am more grateful for all of you than I can possibly say."

"As we are for you, Lady Heloise," the Reverend Halliwell said, giving rise to murmurs of agreement.

For the first time since he'd arrived, Callum Laughlin saw Heloise Somers truly smile. Her cheeks flushed and her teeth flashed, rose-gold eyelashes lowering to hide the pleasure she felt at the compliment.

He had missed that smile. It was enough to light up the entire world.

13

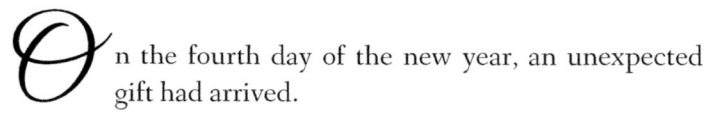

On the fourth day of the new year, an unexpected gift had arrived.

Heloise had been taking stock of one of the damaged houses, making tallies in a ledger, when she was nearly toppled over by a red-faced young man tearing through the township, presumably in search of her. She'd stepped aside just in time to avoid being knocked flat by his speed, allowing him to skid to a halt in the sooty pebbles that made up the pathway.

The lad had regained his footing and his breath, hunched over with a parcel clutched to his middle, and when he raised his head again, she recognized him as the stable boy from the manor house, one of Graham's brood.

She'd held up a hand to silence the admonishments of the two builders she had been surveying alongside that morning, and instead crossed her arms across her chest while awaiting an explanation, one eyebrow quirked with genuine curiosity.

Chapter 13

Robbie thrust out the box he was holding, wrapped in a Moorvale tartan, and as she reached for it, the boy launched into a breathless explanation.

"My sister said this was to go to you straight away, m'Lady, *no delays!*" he exclaimed. "She said she didn't trust Da or Lord Moorvale to deliver it quick enough and that it was *utmost* important."

"Your sister," she repeated curiously. "Do you mean Meggie?"

At the sound of her name, the boy's face lit up in a wide smile. "The very same! She said you'd be wanting these things right away and asked that you write her when you can and let her know how you're coming along. She sent her apologies that she couldn't come down herself, but she's still abed with her new babe."

"Of course she is," Heloise murmured, clutching the box close to her chest. "I have been remiss in my correspondence with Meggie. I must write to her very soon. Thank you, Robbie. Run ahead to the church and my mother will give you a cup of porridge."

She turned to the builders with an apologetic shrug. "Gentlemen, I'm afraid this parcel comes to me with some urgency. I am going to head back to the church to open it. If you would like to join me and take part in some rest and repast, you are more than welcome. We have accomplished quite a bit already this morn."

She had led the way, boots crunching in fresh snowfall as her heart felt light as air in her chest. Meggie would have sent along a midwifery kit, much like the one she'd given Heloise during her training. Inside would be a great many herbs and supplies that would be very useful in the coming days, particularly with Abigail fit to burst at any moment.

Many of the items in the kit would serve as pain relief for some of those who were injured from the fire, and cleansing balms to ward off infection in those who may be at risk of it. She made a mental note to check the laceration above Alex's eye and give more salve to Gloriana so that he might actually stay vigilant in using it.

She chuckled to herself, her breath a little cloud of rising amusement in the morning air. Fate was a funny thing, wasn't it?

Truth be told, she had been in an unusually good mood since awakening after the fire. She had expected a great deal of emotions to come crashing down upon her. All the horrible thoughts she'd had on the night of the disaster seemed to have evaporated with the flames themselves. And the sickening regret she'd expected after her impetuous encounter with Callum Laughlin hadn't yet made itself known, if ever it was going to.

It was the strangest thing, the sense of calm that had overtaken her after that. As ridiculous as it was, and as irrational as their coupling had been, it was as though a tiny piece of her soul had been restored. Perhaps the damage done when she'd thought he could so easily leave her had finally been repaired, regardless of how realistic any actual future with him may or may not be.

He hadn't demanded anything of her since that morning. He hadn't cornered her with expectations or questions, nor had he fallen into obvious brooding or discontent. He had thrown himself into his half of the restoration of the town-

Chapter 13

ship with a work ethic and passion that she felt matched her own, and though they had not had a moment to speak, watching the progress he made and the way the people reacted to him filled her with something perhaps a little more warming than simple respect or gratitude.

Fate indeed had a sense of humor.

Once she'd freed herself of her cloak and gloves, allowing the shiver of warmth to roll over her from the homey embrace of the church, she noticed just how cold she'd gotten. The tip of her nose and the curves of her ears stung with the change in temperature. She suspected there were little flakes of ice on her eyelashes as well.

She wiggled her toes within the stiff confines of her boots and reasoned that at least some of her had stayed warm out there, somehow.

"Ah, the lad gave you the box!" boomed Sheldon Bywater, appearing by her side so quickly that, for the second time that morning, Heloise nearly found herself bowled over. "He was very somber about the task."

"Yes, he was most devoted to delivering it," Heloise agreed, tossing back the tartan blanket that had swaddled the wooden box on its journey to her. "This will assist in the coming days most dearly. I will have to find a suitable gift in return to send to Meggie once we are back to rights around here."

She nodded in the direction which she was headed, to check on Abigail Collins, who lay in her little cot with a book propped on her pregnant belly. Sheldon grinned, shoving his big hands into his jacket pockets, and strode easily alongside her. If they hadn't looked so very different, it would have been easy to imagine him her third brother. He certainly had always played the role well enough.

"Abigail," Heloise said, drawing the other woman's head up from her intent reading. "Have you met Lord Moorvale? He has just arrived with some essential supplies for our rebuilding, and a particular gift to help you and I along in bringing your little one into the world."

Abigail snapped her book shut and straightened, tucking her short brown curls behind her ears. "Pleasure to meet you, my Lord!"

"Likewise," Sheldon agreed. "And might I say, congratulations!"

"Oh." Abigail pinkened, her hand finding the swell of her pregnancy over the blankets. "Thank you so very much."

Heloise hid her smile, perching herself on the foot of Abigail's bed to open the box. Abigail's condition had been no secret amongst the township, but she had stayed hidden since she had begun to show, as to avoid creating awkwardness for herself and her mother amongst the townspeople.

The fire had forced her into the open, where people could see her bright and pink and expecting. Perhaps they would not whisper to each other about the sensibility of shunting the baby off to an orphanage doorstep now that the wee thing was more of a reality to them. Perhaps they would tamper their judgemental imaginations after seeing how close she had come to death.

Hel took her time pushing the box open, savoring it, even though she already knew what was inside. She was greeted with the smell of cedar, just like the scent of her first box,

Chapter 13

which had been lost in the fire. Her heart gave a happy little tug, as though something had been restored to her, despite it all.

She was surprised to find a few items not generally used for midwifery, including a healthy supply of willow bark and a bottle of laudanum for pain as well as a large jar of simple ointment. Meggie truly was a treasure. Inside was a carefully penned note suggesting a mixture of animal fat and the laudanum with a dash of spirits for a burn poultice, to be wrapped in linen.

She inhaled deeply of the cool, late-morning air, closing her eyes to savor this moment of hope. When she opened them, they fell upon her mother, who was ladling the last of the porridge out of a large cauldron at the back of the church.

Ruthie reached out to steady the hands of the old coopmaster, a man of many years whose body had become unwieldy as he'd aged. Together they held the cup still and gently filled it with sustenance, not a drop spilled. She was smiling in a way Heloise rarely saw, allowing the lines that appeared in the corners of her eyes to show. She seemed simpler here, more natural. Even her dress was far less fine than what she'd wear at home. Even when Ruthie was on her knees in the garden, she held up a standard of couture.

Today she was dressed in simple white, silhouetted by the large stained-glass window behind her. She was hardly recognizable as the cynical and brusque Ruthie Cunningham Somers that she'd fashioned herself for Heloise's entire life. She looked like she had cast aside a suit of armor. She looked happy.

Hel's eyes drifted across the room, curious if anyone else

was witnessing this change, and fell upon Reverend Halliwell, who had paused over his folding of freshly washed linens to gaze at her with a sweet little smile on his plain face.

She looked away, back to the box in her hands, feeling as though she had intruded on something preciously private, though she could not say she regretted having seen it.

"You returned very quickly from Scotland," Abigail was saying, her voice a little more breathless than usual in the presence of a great lord.

"Aye, it was hard going," he agreed. "The terrain is piled with ice and even without the road troubles it's colder outside than a witch's ..."

Heloise looked up, raising her eyebrows as her eyes met his.

He hesitated, plastering on an awkward smile, and finished his sentence with, "... heart."

"Indeed," Heloise agreed, stifling her desire to chuckle at his discomfort.

"Might Callum Laughlin stop in soon?" Abigail asked, startling Heloise so much that she almost lost her grip on the box. "I was hoping he might come in for a spot to eat so that I might speak to him."

She turned to look at her charge, whose eyes had grown wide and dreamy.

"It's only that I never thanked him for saving me," she explained, a blush spreading to her cheeks. "We were sweethearts when we were young, you know."

"Were you indeed?" Sheldon chuckled. "Then I'm sure your

husband is none too pleased at Laughlin's heroism recapturing your attentions."

"Oh," Abby whispered. "No, m'Lord."

A silence fell over the three of them as Abigail lowered her eyes and Sheldon looked from woman to woman in hapless confusion at what faux pas he had just made. Heloise wasn't about to humiliate her charge with the announcement that she was indeed unmarried, and instead pushed herself to her feet with a somewhat forced, but cheery countenance.

"I'm going to take this over to my new sister-in-law and have her add it to our list of medical supplies," she announced. "Abigail, might I bring you anything? Porridge?"

"No, m'Lady," she said softly. "I ate already and am well stuck into this story you lent me. Hopefully I'll finish it before the babe comes and I have no time for such things anymore."

"Well, then I will leave you to it," she said, gathering up the box, but leaving the tartan in case Abigail desired some extra warmth. "I will be back to check on you in a little bit."

Across the room, Gloriana was devising some new distraction for a gaggle of village children who seemed to flock to her the way moths are entranced by a flame in the dark. She became very animated when instructing them on some new task to distract them with, and then as soon as they were gone, she always flopped forward into her hands as though she needed to gather her strength again.

Heloise arrived at just this moment, lifting the box over her head as the village children hurried past her in a horde of giggles.

Gloriana peeked up through her fingers, her pale blue eyes catching the sunlight as she saw Heloise approach. "Do you recall," she asked, "that morning that you told me you were not experiencing schadenfreude at my expense?"

"Of course I do." Heloise grinned. "It was only a couple of months ago."

"I suspect that you are experiencing said phenomenon right now instead," Gloriana told her, then leaned back to stretch her arms over her head. "I do not know how I became the pied piper of children."

"It is because you're beautiful and you were wearing that lavish silver dress on the night of the fire. Children are simple creatures, easily enchanted." Heloise set the midwifery box on the desk Gloriana was seated before and laid a freckled hand upon it. "But, if it helps, I have brought a distraction—much-needed medical supplies to add to our stockpile."

"Medical supplies?" Gloriana repeated, furrowing her brow. "But Rose said not to expect them back for another week at least."

"This is a midwife's box," Hel explained, lifting the lid. "The woman who apprenticed me has sent it down from Moorvale to replace the one I lost in the fire. It is primarily filled with supplies for women's matters, but there is plenty in here that can assist the others, including ingredients for a soothing burn poultice."

Gloriana's pale, unblemished fingers passed over Hel's freckled ones, moving a few items around to get a look inside the box. "I've no idea what most of this is," she confessed, brushing against a parcel of herbs. "You will have to help me index it."

"Of course."

Gloriana looked up, catching her lip between her teeth. She seemed to weigh her desire to speak against her hesitation to do so, and then all at once blurted out, "I don't suppose we could go over it back at Somerton in a few hours?"

"Together?" Heloise asked, unable to hide the surprise in her voice.

Gloriana reached from the box over to Hel's hand, gripping it lightly in her own. "Please. I'm desperate to get out of this church for a bit. Besides, it will be easier and cleaner to spread out all the contents of your box back there."

"I do need to go back and check on the children," Heloise replied, mostly to amuse herself at the way Gloriana flinched at the idea of yet more children. "If you give me an hour or so, we might ride back together and take a light lunch. We ought to compare our ledgers anyhow."

Gloriana nodded, a strand of platinum hair escaping her bun and drifting down over her cheek. She did not seem to feel it and sighed a little gust of fatigue. "Perhaps we will have some tiny sandwiches?" she suggested hopefully. "Cucumber, perhaps? Cheese?"

"I will see that we have the tiniest of sandwiches," she assured her.

As she walked away from that particular encounter, Hel thought for the third time in one morning that fate must laugh merrily at the machinations of all the silly humans in her thrall.

14

To Heloise's genuine astonishment, Gloriana suggested they ride horseback to Somerton rather than take a carriage.

"Better a quick blast of cold than shambling along in it," she said. "Besides, I know you hate the carriage."

It was just as well. On horseback, bundled against the elements, they were not required to attempt small talk with one another. While their youthful rivalry had dissolved into little more than an embarrassing memory, they were not yet what one could call friends.

Alex loved Gloriana and Heloise loved her brother, which was enough to end her long-held dislike for the effortless beauty and grace embodied by the girl who never seemed to want for anything. In truth, it was a shock that Glory had been the one to insist on staying at Somerton rather than departing for her long-planned honeymoon abroad. She had allowed her wedding dress to be destroyed by all those little sooty handprints. She had worked herself

Chapter 14

through to the dawn on what should have been her wedding night.

Even without everything else, that would have earned Heloise's respect. The Gloriana she thought she'd known in her youth, during those stifled days at Mrs. Arlington's, would have thrown a tantrum at the prospect of her perfect wedding day and subsequent tour of Europe being interrupted, no matter by what.

It was only snowing in light flurries, but the speed of the horses meant that they caught enough snowflakes to crust them both in crystals by the time they reached the Somerton stables. Though her face was wrapped in a scarf, Heloise was grinning broadly beneath it. Rides like this one were always invigorating.

They dismounted, Glory handing her reins off to a wide-eyed Robbie, who was somewhere between that childhood enchantment that the village children had experienced and the dumbfounded attraction that grown men seemed to topple into when Gloriana was present. For once, it did not irk Heloise.

She shook her hair out, scratching Boudicea fondly between the eyes, and glanced at the stalls while Robbie saw to Glory's horse. That speckled black and white stallion she'd seen the night of the fire was there again, this time far less agitated, but clearly curious and alert, leaning against his stall to get a better look at them.

"Robbie, when did we acquire that stallion?" she asked, pointing. "He is very fine indeed, but I do not recall anyone mentioning him to me."

"That's because he's mine," answered Callum Laughlin,

striding into the stables with the easy confidence of a man who once called them home. He flashed them a smile, his teeth bright and eyes sparkling in the sunlight as he came closer. "His name is Caesar."

Heloise managed a little laugh, despite the way her stomach had lurched up into her chest at his appearance. "Of course it is," she said, handing Boudicea's reins to Robbie. "I ought to have known."

He looked down on her with knowing in his eyes, that smile lingering on his lips. He looked vibrant and energized, the way he always had when she'd interrupted him at his work. It made her heart thud rather obstinately against her chest.

"Will you join us for lunch, Lieutenant?" Gloriana asked, clearly ready to head indoors and make use of the fire. "We are going to check in on the children and compare our numbers for the township. I imagine you might have some useful input."

Reluctantly, Callum tore his dark eyes from Heloise. When he looked at Glory, he did not freeze or gawk or leer. He looked upon her as if she were any woman with whom he had polite but disinterested acquaintance. From his expression and unconcerned posture, she might have been a grandmother with a bent back and rheumy eyes rather than the toast of London. Could it truly be that he was unaffected by her beauty?

"Unfortunately, I am only here to change out the cookware at my mother's behest," he said with a friendly nod. "But I very much appreciate the invitation. Which children do you speak of? I'm afraid I have not had the pleasure of

Chapter 14

meeting any within the manor. Does Viscount Somers already have an heir or two?"

"He has been four years married," Heloise reminded him, aware that her voice suddenly sounded somewhat choked. It was no accident that he had not seen hide nor hair of the children within the estate. She busied herself removing her gloves to avoid meeting his eye, lest she give herself away. "Gideon's son is named Reginald, after Glory's father. Our viscountess is very fond of her uncle and insisted on the tribute. We call him Reggie."

"The other is a relation from the Americas," Glory added, hugging her elbows against the cold. "A little girl who was sadly orphaned and now is ward to the Somers family. She is very dear."

Callum shook his head in wonder. "Much has changed in my absence."

"We must catch you up someday soon," Glory said with a tight smile. "But I'm afraid Lady Heloise and I must needs head inside before we turn to ice."

"I was hoping to steal a moment of Lady Heloise's time," he said apologetically. "It will only take a few minutes, but it is rather urgent."

"Here," Hel said, holding out the box. "Go inside and get warm. Order up those sandwiches, and I will join you shortly."

Gloriana approached, taking the box from Heloise, her eyes keen and questioning, as though to make sure Heloise truly wished to be left alone in the stables with the handsome lieutenant. Hel gave a little nod and what she hoped was an encouraging quirk of the lips in response.

"Thank you," Glory said, suddenly airy and careless. "I am just hopeless in the cold! Until we next meet, Lieutenant."

"My pleasure, Lady Somers."

Glory flushed in pleasure at her new title and spun away, making a quick exit from the stables and leaving Hel and Callum in a sudden vacuum of quiet, with only the sound of Robbie brushing the horses interrupting the silence.

When she was certain Glory had gone, and was definitely within the manor house, she grabbed Callum's arm and marched him across the stables and beneath the loft, into a corner where they would not be overheard by the enthusiastic stable boy. He came along easily, seemingly pleased to be touched by her in any context whatsoever.

She took a bracing breath, turning her head up to meet his eyes in a shadowy alcove framed with horseshoes. "I owe you an apology," she said softly.

He laughed, a sudden burst of amusement that had Heloise shushing him with a paranoid look around for eavesdroppers. "I'm sorry," he chuckled, lowering his voice. "But you most certainly do *not*."

"Callum!" she hissed, giving him a light shove. "Be serious, please."

"I am serious," he said, that chuckle still on his breath as he gripped the hand she'd placed against his chest. "I know it was a fraught moment and that neither of us were thinking clearly, but I could no more regret touching you again than I could regret drawing breath. I hope you do not begrudge me that."

She watched him, wary as a doe, but did not snatch her hand away. He was holding it against his heart, which she could feel through the layers of winter clothing as though it were tuned like an orchestra in tandem with her own.

"I am the one who owes you an apology," he continued, his voice deeper. He took a step closer to her, their breath mingling against the cold air. "I realize now how thoughtless I was and what I must do to make it right."

"What must you do?" she breathed, wishing she could control the way her skin erupted in a thousand dancing flames which burned hotter the closer he got.

He rubbed his thumb along the back of her hand. Such a small motion that sent a molten rush through her very core. "I have never taken the time to woo you, as you deserve," he told her. "I have been presumptuous and inconsiderate and did not know how lucky I was that you took the reins all those years ago."

"Did I?" she said, biting her lip. "I seem to recall you initiating our kiss in the stables."

"The first one was you," he reminded her. "Some three years prior, after you broke my arm. I only wished to improve upon it."

"I didn't break your arm!" she tutted, giving another little shove with her captive hand and making him grin broadly. "You entered every caper willingly, sir."

"And I'd do so again," he told her, lowering his forehead to meet hers. "In an instant."

She let her eyes flutter shut, knowing she should flee, that she shouldn't let this happen as it was. How could she, when it felt so very, very good having him near again? How could she when all she wanted to do was collapse into his arms and beg him to carry her to his bed?

"Heloise," he whispered. "I want to deserve you."

Damn him.

She wrapped her free arm around his neck, pulling him tight against her body as she pressed her lips into his. He kissed her softly, sweetly. It was nothing of the urgent, hungry way they had kissed before. Even during that enchanted summer she could not recall him being so gentle with her.

He was the one who pulled back, releasing her hand in favor of stroking the side of her face. "You are so beautiful." He sighed. "I have to force myself not to watch you at every moment in that church. It has been a torment to be able to see you and not touch you."

"Callum ..." she murmured helplessly.

"Shh," he said, kissing her on either cheek. "We will talk later. Go warm yourself, have your meal. Huddling you into a dank corner of a wooden stable is not how I intend to court you."

"Court me?" she echoed, her voice small and befuddled.

He smoothed her cloak for her and stepped away with a gentlemanly bow. "I will take my leave, Lady Heloise."

She opened her mouth but no response came out. She found herself quite stuck in her position for a length of time

Chapter 14

she would never be certain of before she shook herself and headed indoors.

---

*S*he found Gloriana in the drawing room, curled on the couch with Nero on one side and Callie on the other, both asleep. A platter of half-eaten finger foods was atop the table before them next to a neatly arranged emptying of Meggie's box.

Little Reggie had taken himself to the windowed corner of the room, where he appeared to be attempting to chew the head off a very expensive-looking wooden horse. Everyone seemed quite unconcerned with one another until Heloise interrupted their peace.

Gloriana looked up, her fingers still stroking Callie's ringlets. "That was more than a brief moment," she said. "I have unpacked the box, and am currently guarding it from our resident imp."

Callie yawned, her big black eyes blinking open, and smiled up at her mother. "Auntie Hel."

"Caroline," Heloise replied, unable to resist reaching forward to stroke her cheek. "Did you have a pleasant nap?"

"No nap!" Reggie cried from his perch, which startled the cat awake as well. He slammed the very slobbery horse onto the floor and reiterated, "Hate naps!"

Nero leapt off the couch and darted off to find silence elsewhere, his indignation apparent.

"May I play with Reggie?" Callie asked, seemingly unperturbed by the outburst from her rambunctious cousin.

"Of course you may," Glory cooed. "But perhaps choose a different toy for yourself, all right? That little horse looks rather worse for the wear."

Callie nodded obediently and slid off the couch, smoothing her hands down her little skirt as she trotted off to join her cousin.

Both women watched her go, amazed at how well the two took to one another, despite their opposing personalities. Heloise stepped forward to settle next to Gloriana on the couch and reached forward to retrieve one of the little sandwiches from the platter.

"He is Callie's father, isn't he? The lieutenant."

Hel froze, the sandwich midway to her mouth, her eyes snapping over to her nemesis turned sister-in-law. "What did you say?"

Glory giggled, shaking her head. "He is *very* handsome, Heloise. If I weren't hopelessly in love with Alex, I might find myself rather jealous."

"Of *me?*" Hel choked, giving up and dropping the sandwich into her lap.

"Mm, the way he watches you ... like you're a goddess." She flashed a little smile, conspiratorial and knowing. "It must be intoxicating."

"I don't know where you got the impression that Caroline is—"

Gloriana held her hand up, waving away the protestation as

though it were an irritating gnat. "I wish I could say it was a great deal of cleverness and detective work on my part," she confessed, "but his initials match the inscription in the book, and the child has your chin and his eyes. *And* you fled Mrs. Arlington's so suddenly and all on your own. It doesn't take a genius to put it all together, which is well, because I am not one."

"You mustn't tell Alex," Heloise whispered. "I never revealed who the father was."

"But he knows the child is yours?" she said with a tilt of her head. "How curious. He would never have told me, I think."

"He loves you," Heloise said miserably. "His loyalty to me shouldn't compromise that. And now both you and Rose must keep my secret from your husbands, for they must not know."

"You told Rose?"

"She guessed, on the night I gave birth. I was too spent to attempt a deception." She pinched the bridge of her nose, squeezing her eyes shut against the swell of panic that had begun to subside. "You know, many midwives will demand the name of the father from an unattached mother at the moment of birth. It is said that during such pain, a woman has no will to lie."

Gloriana shuddered. "I have been meaning to speak to you about that."

"About what?" Hel said, dropping her hand and turning to her new sister. "You've not yet been married a week."

"Well, exactly," Gloriana said, delicately reaching for a cloth napkin and handing it to Hel, who had rather soiled her skirt with her dropped sandwich. "I am wondering if there is a way to ... to postpone conception, just until I am ready to be a mother, you understand."

Heloise raised her eyebrows. It was not the first time she had been asked such a question, but it was the first time it had been posed by a woman who was as yet childless. The fact that Gloriana would trust her with such an inquiry was a shock. It would be quite scandalous if anyone were to catch wind that she was not eager to have as many babies as possible. In fact, it was shocking enough to strip her of any of her concern over the revelation of Callie's paternity.

"I imagine you learned of such things after falling victim to pregnancy yourself," Gloriana continued, her voice taking on an anxious quality. "So that it would not happen again?"

"The most effective way is simply to avoid the marital bed," Heloise said. "That is the advice most midwives would give you."

Gloriana winced, averting her eyes. "No."

Heloise found herself giggling. She never giggled, but such a flat refusal to give up the pleasures of the boudoir struck her on such a relatable level that she had to turn her head to stifle her laughter. Perhaps it was a touch of hysteria, an outlet of the multiple shocks she'd had over the last hour.

The realization that she had already compromised herself again and could at this very moment be once again with child out of wedlock was deeply amusing to her for some reason, combined with the content of this conversation. Luckily, Gloriana simply looked bashful, as though the amusement had come completely from her own admission of wantonness.

She calmed herself, dabbing at the corners of her eyes, and breathed out a steadying gust of breath. "There are a few tricks that work for some women, but nothing is guaranteed. A rinse of oil prior to ... erm, the act," she said, stifling another hiccup of laughter, "is the one I've heard is most effective. Some women use a bit of sponge on a string as a barrier, and of course there is the technique that brothels employ."

"Brothels?" Gloriana breathed, fluttering her lashes. "What do you know of brothels?"

"Plenty," Heloise laughed. "Those women are in need of my services perhaps more than any family in town. It is not as scandalously fun as it sounds, I assure you."

"And what do these women do?" she asked, scooting closer, her pale blue eyes wide with curiosity.

She sighed, glancing over her shoulder to ensure the children could not hear them.

This was not a conversation she thought she would be having with Gloriana Blakely, now or ever. Even so, it was her duty to give advice such as this to those who asked, free of judgement or admonishment. "It is mostly to prevent disease," she explained, "which you need not concern yourself with. What they do is employ a length of cured intestine, usually from a sheep, to make a sort of sheath. The man wears it, inflated first and then secured with a ribbon over his ... his organ, protecting each partner from the risks of the other."

Glory blinked and then sat back, a dazed look on her face.

"I will show you how to track your fertility by your monthly cycle, so that you may avoid the riskiest days of each month," Heloise said, "though again, I must emphasize that nothing is a certain prevention."

"What if ..." Glory swallowed, turning her eyes up to the ceiling, her voice growing thin. "What if he spills his seed elsewhere?"

Heloise coughed, wishing this conversation were about any man other than her brother, but did her best to retain the cool professionalism she'd learned to maintain in even the most dire of circumstances. If she could manage the blood and pain of the childbed, she could certainly have a civilized conversation about its mechanics. "It will reduce your chances of conception, certainly, but ... erm, traces of a man's seed are present throughout the act, from the beginning."

The two sat in silence for a moment after that, each opting to turn their heads and stare forward at the opposite wall rather than to look at one another or speak. A beat of silence was just the thing to ease the awkwardness in the room.

"I simply wish to enjoy being a newlywed first," Glory finally whispered, embarrassment clear in her voice. "I do not feel prepared to be a mother. Perhaps I never will."

"If you do have a child," Heloise said, turning back and reaching across the couch to touch her hand, "you will not be alone and you will not be adrift. And, once you've conceived, so long as you produce mother's milk, you will remain infertile, so if you wish to stop at one, that is a way to do so."

Gloriana gave a skeptical look down at her modest bosom.

Chapter 14

"Hopefully we don't have to get that far, for I would be a paltry wet nurse indeed," she sighed, gripping Heloise's hand back. "Thank you. I know I do not deserve such kindness after the ways I've misused you."

Heloise laughed again, that bubble of hysteria reappearing, buoyant in her chest. "Glory, I dyed your teeth purple. Your occasional cutting comments over tea hardly compare. Between us, consider yourself to have the moral high ground."

Gloriana giggled, raising a hand to cover her mouth, as though her teeth still had the ink imprinted upon them. "You did, didn't you?"

For the remainder of the afternoon, as they worked their way through inventories and costs, neither woman had much success at stifling the little bursts of laughter, inspired by the conversation they'd just endured.

15

The coop and kennel were nearly finished.

As it happened, animal homes were much easier to rebuild than those occupied by man. The only thing slowing them down was how quickly the cold seeped into one's bones out in the Yorkshire chill, and how easy it was for a man to be oblivious to his body slowly being taken by the icy fingers of winter.

Callum had instituted a rotation, pulling the men in to warm up in shifts so that the work would progress but no one would lose fingers to frostbite. He wished he could avoid his own time in the church, allowing the stinging prickles of warmth to permeate his clammy skin and reawaken the nerves and blood within, but of course he couldn't undermine his own orders.

It wasn't the physical discomfort. It was a thousand irritants within the crush of bodies in the church and a disappointing lack of Heloise Somers to brighten the interlude. She had been much at work within the manor for the last

Chapter 15

week, writing letters, meeting with laborers, drafting estimates, and such.

Some supplies had arrived from Leeds and York, but they were incomplete and the members of the family who had gone to get them had been waylaid by inclement travel conditions, which left it to Heloise to decide their next steps. To her credit, she didn't falter once she'd made a decision.

Callum had no head for numbers, but apparently both Hel and the new Somers bride had been trained in exacting detail of how to squeeze every pence to its last drop of copper.

He had always known she was remarkable, but she continued to surprise him by the day. He had been sending her notes, scribbled in his unrefined hand, with stories of the times he thought of her during the war and what a pleasure it was to see her now in truth. He would describe the way the sunlight had caught her hair or the way her voice gave him pause.

He knew where a few wildflowers still grew in the dead of winter. Sturdy blooms of purple and yellow and pink that sprung from the snow in the hidden corners of the moor. He plucked them when he could and folded at least one into each of his letters. Each letter and flower had one more element—his *coup de grâce*—one of the four-year-old notes she'd written him, from that summer they'd had together, tucked into the center.

He'd kept them all, of course, pressed between pages of the books he carried. He'd read the short, often single-sentence messages over and over, especially in the darkest of times.

He told her he was only returning them to her because she had lent him her spirit, and now that he was able to see her again, he was no longer in need of the favor.

It amused him how obviously uncomfortable she was with formal courting. He loved the way her eyes narrowed and her lips pursed when he insisted on being perfectly genteel, kissing her hand and nothing more, even when they could not possibly have been observed. When he suggested they attend a ball together in the spring, she had actually thrown up her hands and stalked away from him, muttering to herself.

Perhaps his attempts at formal wooing were not particularly up to par with a practiced man of the gentry, but he knew Heloise hated everything about being a member of the peerage anyhow. The point wasn't to irritate her, of course, it was to show her that she was worth waiting for. He hoped she understood that, even if he had begun to take a little bit of enjoyment out of her ongoing befuddlement.

He hoped she knew that beneath all his propriety, there was still a great deal of heat. Did she suspect how difficult it was for him to sleep when he remembered her astride him in that ruin? Did she gather how much restraint it took not to whisk her off into the nearest nook when she looked at him with heat in her eyes, fingering one of the flowers he'd given her as she gazed at him from across a room? It was the only thing keeping his blood hot in this frigid climate.

It wasn't ideal that the only time of day he was guaranteed to see her was when she came into the church to perform her midwife duties. Aside from being an inappropriate time for flirtation on principle, Abby Collins went moon-eyed every time he came into the building. He didn't want to

Chapter 15

encourage it, but he knew he'd be an awful person if he pretended not to see or hear her calling out to him when he was near.

There was something strange about having eyelashes batted at you by a woman whose belly was full of someone else's baby. He couldn't decide if it was flattering or upsetting. She had been a fun and carefree young woman when last he'd seen her, but they'd never shared any true intimacy beyond the physical, no emotional connection that might account for the way she clung to him like a long-lost kindred spirit.

Heloise had never commented upon it, and he had not been able to read her face when the three of them happened to collide. He suspected she had a variety of thoughts on the matter that he would not particularly enjoy.

In any event, Heloise's presence was a rarity in the church when she was not midwifing, and their chance encounters in the village were not much more frequent.

When he had his breaks from rebuilding, forced into the church to return warmth to his bones, he often paced the perimeters, uncertain what to do with himself. It had been a distressingly frequent frame of mind since his return to Britain.

Everyone he knew by name was thoroughly occupied if they were in the sanctuary when he was. The reverend was always busy with something, often managing stacks of cycled clothing, cleaning, and dispensing to the masses, or otherwise enclosed in his office, frantically attempting to revise and index the town records.

Callum found that much like the dowager viscountess,

Reverend Halliwell looked as though he hadn't aged in all of Callum's life, but instead existed in a perpetual suspension of elderhood. It was comforting, he decided, to find some things unchanged.

The innkeeper had badly burned the lower half of one of his legs on the night of the fire and did occasionally indulge Callum in some casual conversation, when he was up to it. Today he seemed to be dozing off, his damaged leg freshly wrapped in a red-tinted set of bandages. Callum hesitated to approach him only because the town physician, the man he was certain was sniffing after Heloise, was currently inspecting the dressings on the innkeeper's leg.

The doctor caught his eye before he could feign intent in a different direction and gave a pleasant nod and smile of acknowledgement. He gestured to the dressing, encouraging Callum to come nearer, and said, "It is quite something, is it not? An ingenious method of numbing the pain. My only concern is that keeping the area moist might delay healing."

Callum nodded, remembering the triage tents he'd seen on the coast and the makeshift comforts far from trained medics. He could almost smell the sizzle of flesh and the clouds of gunpowder escaping from the memory.

"I have seen burns treated both ways, in the field," the doctor continued. "Some insist on drying it out and allowing a scab to do the work, while others insist that moisture saps away the damage. I can't say I have any concrete conclusions on the matter."

"We kept them covered, on the Continent," Callum replied,

Chapter 15

for lack of anything else to say. "But our resources were scarce."

"Yes, and I imagine there was nothing much to assist with the pain. It is fascinating. I have never used laudanum topically," the doctor mused, tapping his chin thoughtfully and glancing up at Callum as though he might have some opinion on the matter, simply on merit of him standing nearby. "It is shocking sometimes how tidbits of genius emerge from midwifery. It would shock the average man to his bones!"

"Of course. It is an ancient and respected practice," Callum said, though the doctor appeared not to realize such a basic fact. Callum cleared his throat, not wishing to offend the man, and attempted to shift the subject. "I notice that you leave the care of Miss Collins entirely to Lady Heloise. You must respect her skill a great deal to allow her to shoulder the full care of a vulnerable woman that way."

The doctor gave a tight little smile at the mention of Heloise.

He knows I'm a threat, Callum realized. *He still wants her.*

"Male midwives are a perverse thing, Lieutenant. Very much fringe medicine and highly suspect in educated circles," the doctor informed him with a sniff and an aversion of his eyes, as though this were distasteful to even mention. "A true gentleman of learning would distance himself far from interference in that particular domain, and as such, *matters* of the female condition are not my rightful occupation. I rather think Miss Collins would do well to avoid being alone with men for a while anyway, wouldn't you say?"

Callum blinked in surprise. "I'm certain no one would consider consultation with a physician amiss. Do you not monitor the health of expecting mothers in the township?"

"Best not to risk it," the doctor said, shrugging, "especially with a chit like that. Even after she has the babe, it will be well known that she is open for compromise. Best to avoid any possibility of scandal or entrapment."

"Entrapment?" Callum repeated, but Dr. Garber was already patting him on the shoulder and moving on to his next patient.

"Lovely to talk to you, Lieutenant. Let's share a drink sometime soon. I must finish my rounds."

He watched him go with his brow still furrowed. Did he think that giving medical attention to an unwed mother would somehow snare him into being forced to step in and marry the poor woman? Surely that was not the case. He was certain the old physician had attended to women alongside their midwives.

Callum glanced over at Abigail with a frown. He realized that she never had anyone attending her other than her mother and Heloise. The townspeople drifted past her as though they could not see her at all. He stood for a moment, as though to confirm he wasn't imagining things. It took no time at all to witness the phenomenon directly. He watched it happen, noted the way people deliberately turned away from her, as though even looking at her might taint them.

Abby didn't seem to notice, tucked into the novels Heloise had lent her. Or perhaps she knew very well what was happening and had decided it was better overall simply to ignore it, just like they ignored her. He suddenly felt a

Chapter 15

swell of guilt for begrudging her his company. They had once been a sort of friends, after all, even if it had been shallow.

He remained unsullied, he realized, despite his youthful indiscretions.

Even back then, he supposed, she'd had a reputation. She often told him with a sigh and a shrug that her mother had told her so many times that she would never marry that it was bound to come true. He had been a fool then, young and full of distracting thoughts about girls and their many, many temptations, so rather than respond or ask after her well-being, he had simply wished to return to whatever dabbling in physicality they had been most recently engaged in.

The summer that Heloise had come home, he had stopped visiting the township. He had no use for village girls when Lady Heloise had deemed him worthy of her touch. His sudden disappearance must have been hurtful, he realized, if Abigail thought him a true friend or a caring one.

He straightened his shoulders and took a determined stride over to her cot. He allowed the whispering townspeople to make way for him instead of bothering to be concerned with where they chose to stand. He arrived with purpose, cutting a path through the whisperers, and plopped himself down on the bed at her feet.

"Lieutenant," she said in surprise, clapping her book shut and straightening herself. "Are you looking for Lady Heloise?"

"No," Callum said, that pang of guilt ringing again in his chest. "I am simply warming my bones for an hour before resuming the building. I was hoping you might lend me the pleasure of your conversation while I thaw."

The swell of whispers and glances in their direction was ostensible. It turned that pang of guilt into a little flame of anger. After all, if the stars had aligned differently, it might have been he who put her in this situation, just as guilty as she. Would he have been hiding in that crowd, joining in the whispers? Would he have married her? He did not know.

Her pretty face blossomed into the most brilliant smile. She set the book aside, tucking her short hair behind her ears. "I would love to," she replied. "I have very much missed simple conversation."

16

Returning to Somerton via the front door was something he still wasn't quite adapted to. The instinctive steps from the stable toward the kitchen entrance caught him every time. Caesar had come to expect a second passing-by of his master, and an additional pat on the head at night as Callum rerouted himself into the manor proper.

He almost always arrived home later than the others who were sleeping abovestairs. He took care with his movements, not wishing to disturb anyone, even the occasional maid he passed in the dark. He found that after the first couple of times, he did not need to bother with a lantern to find his new room.

Perhaps he was adapting to luxury faster than he realized. He certainly knew he'd never be satisfied with a hay-stuffed mattress again, at the very least.

He could hear the wind howling outside. Some of the men

had predicted a squall blowing in after sunset, and it seemed they were correct. Callum only hoped the gales didn't disturb any of the unfinished construction and undo days and days of work.

He pushed the door to his bedroom open, his hand already going for the tinderbox and lantern on the side table when he blinked a few times, realizing that the room was already awash with candlelight and the crackle of a fire in the hearth.

He froze, turning his head toward the intruder, a bored-looking Heloise Somers, lounging in one of the arm chairs with her foot propped up on the ottoman. She had a stack of loose papers next to her that she had seemingly discarded, and the core of an apple sat on the table to her left. He wondered if she'd been working through reconstruction administration while she waited for him.

She didn't rise or acknowledge his entry other than meeting his eyes across the room, a smug little smile curling the corners of her lips. She was wearing a simple, navy-colored sheath dress and her glorious mane of hair was loose down her back, with only the sides curled back and pinned behind her ears. He noted, as quickly and discreetly as possible, the line of her bare calf that was visible from the angle of the foot she was resting aloft with its little silk slipper dangling off her heel.

He hadn't seen the lines of her body so clearly since the morning of the wedding breakfast. Even when they'd had their moment of indiscretion, she had been layered against the cold. Probably best not to dwell upon that thought too long.

Chapter 16

"I suppose I shouldn't ask how or why you came to find your way into my room," he finally said, shrugging off his jacket and making his way to the coat stand. Seeing her relaxed on that chair without her layers and layers of winter-wear, beyond providing a particularly pleasing tableau, made him wish to shed all of his bulky outdoor wear as well. Was there anything so luxurious as kicking off one's boots after putting them to use all day?

"This is my childhood home," she replied easily. "I will find my way into whichever rooms I please with very little trouble."

"Well, it's hardly appropriate," he said with mock sternness. "Surely I should ring for a chaperone."

She rolled her eyes, slinging her feet from the ottoman to the ground, and pushed herself to her feet. "Yes, yes, you've made your point quite well. You're a true gentleman now, starch and all. I am convinced, despite the quality of the poetry."

"It wasn't poetry," Callum replied with a lift of his chin. "I didn't create rhymes."

She laughed, tossing her hair over her shoulder and stalking toward him the way one might imagine a lioness approaching her prey. She drew herself up a breath away from him, tilting her head up to meet his eye, and said with a cryptic little grin, "I heard about what you did today."

"Finishing the chicken coop?" he guessed.

"No, but allow me to express extreme praise for that as well," she said with a sincere lift of her brows. "However, I am speaking of your display of friendship to Abby Collins. You set the church marms into quite the indignant buzz. Don't you know you're supposed to shun her completely? Don't you know they were enjoying their laughter at the way she gazes at you?"

"I've never made a very good church marm," he replied. "Though I am sorry to hear I was the cause of mockery at her expense."

Heloise scoffed, waving a hand as though to dispel the memory of such people. "If it weren't you, it would've been some other peevish nonsense. The important thing is that today, you managed to not only silence them, but cause them a degree of shame at their behavior. In a church of all places, one should extend kindness to the less fortunate."

He hesitated, uncertain what exactly was happening, searching the merry sparkle in her emerald eyes for some clue as to what he was supposed to do next. Uncertainly, he attempted, "I hope you do not think I was encouraging any romantic attachment through my company. I simply wished to provide her with a degree of friendship where she seems to have very little."

She narrowed her eyes a little, as though she were searching for his intentions as well. "I know that, you fool man," she snapped, though there was no sharpness to her words. "Why do you think I came here? To scold you?"

So powerful was the urge to pull her against him and plunder the petulant softness of her pretty mouth that he forced himself to swallow and take a step backward. "I wouldn't presume such assumptions, Lady Heloise."

Chapter 16

"Lady Heloise," she mocked in a particularly poor imitation of his voice. "You are toying with me, Callum. Why?"

He chuckled despite himself, and held his hands up in surrender at her incensed expression. "I wasn't intending to, truly. It was only that once I realized how much it flustered you, it was too endearing to stop. Did you enjoy the bad poetry, at the very least, even as comedy?"

She crossed her arms and looked away, appearing very close to a pout. There was his impetuous Heloise, hidden under all those layers of sensible adulthood. "You know very well I did," she huffed. "I can't believe you kept all those stupid notes. I was such a little fool."

"You were many things," he replied, unable to resist reaching forward for her, pulling her closer with one arm wrapped around her slender waist, touching the tip of his nose to hers. "You are still. Not a fool, though."

She shivered, biting down on her lip and letting her eyelids flutter shut. "I'm still a fool," she confessed, tracing the flats of her palms up along his chest and looping them around his neck. "It's all your fault."

He brushed the stubbled edge of his cheek against the silken line of her jaw. He dropped light kisses on her cheek, at the tip of her sharp little chin, into the hollow at the top of her throat. "I certainly hope so," he whispered into the warmth of that delicate skin. "I'd feared I had no effect on you at all."

"Then you are a fool as well," she breathed, melting into him, the heat of her body radiating through the thin material of her dress. "I think you know very well why I came here and what I want."

If she was hoping that he would be the one to think clearly, to put a stop to this, she was making it less likely by the second. He ran his hands down her sides, his thumbs teasing at the sides of her breasts, the dip of her waist. He slid his workman's fingers over the pert little swell of her bottom and pulled her hips into his, his arousal pressing into the soft sweetness of her belly. He held her there, allowing her to feel how very much he wanted the same things she alluded to, and met her gaze, his eyes hot and gleaming.

She met that gaze, fearless and challenging as ever. "I took precautions," she said softly, trailing a finger down the center of his chest, "but you must withdraw from me before you spend your seed. Can you do that?"

He nodded, certain the movement was more curt than the situation demanded, but he could hardly think for the things her words had put into his mind. His ears were nigh ringing because of it.

She smiled then, the devilish little grin of a born troublemaker, and pressed the tip of her finger into his chest, just above his heart, pushing herself a step away. "Good," she said. "Lock the door."

He did not hesitate, turning on his heel and snatching the room key from its place on the table with the tinderbox. He turned the lock into place, securing them into the room together, and turned around to find the wind nearly knocked out of him.

She was, somehow, already nude, standing in the puddle of fabric that had been her dress. She had her arms hanging at her sides, her chin raised, hair like glowing magma spilling down her back and twining over the lean muscles of her freckled arms. She was lit from behind by the fire, the rise and fall of her breath giving the only hint that she was not an apparition nor sculpture.

He allowed his eyes to scrape over her, to indulge in the visual feast that she presented, which he had been able to only conjure from memory for such a very, very long time. Had she grown more lush in his absence? Her hips seemed rounder, softer somehow. Her breasts looked fuller and heavier.

He found himself pulling his own shirt off over his head, tossing it away in some unknown direction. He did not know if she had pictured him in his absence or if women found as much pleasure in the male form as the latter did the former, but he wanted to give her everything and more that she was willing to give to him.

He rose from removing his trousers, just as bare as she, and stood opposite the firelight. There was a flicker of satisfaction in him at the way her eyes roamed over the broad muscle of his chest, lingering on a few of the scars he had acquired since she had last seen him. As her gaze lowered, her tongue darted out and moistened her lips, likely unaware of just how provocative such a motion was.

He didn't trust himself to touch her. He didn't trust himself to do anything that he wanted this much and not somehow muck it up. Still, as those eyes rose to find his again, he couldn't help crossing the divide between them. He couldn't resist her any more than the seasons could resist changing, any more than the sun could cease to dance with the moon.

She dug her fingers into his hair, dragging his mouth down to meet hers as he lifted her from the floor, wrapping her legs around his middle. He carried her without interrupting her kiss, to the luxurious bed in the center of the room—a far cry from the hayloft they once shared. He lowered her gently onto the coverlet, bracing one arm and then the other on either side of her so that he would not have to let her go completely.

He only left the sweetness of her mouth to explore elsewhere, to kiss down to the elegant lines of her collar, the tops of those beautiful breasts. He flicked his tongue against the rosy delicacy of her nipples, basking in the sound of her quickening breath. He slid his fingers down over the soft planes of her belly, the indents along her hipbones, his hands roaming to the places he'd long wished to revisit. He separated her thighs and stroked the silky skin just below where they met as his lips trailed down to follow the path his hands had taken.

In the dancing shadows of the firelight, her skin appeared at once a single pale slate of alabaster, void of her freckling in some places, while wild and spotted as a fawn's in others. His fingers traced over three silver lines on her hip, perhaps a scar from some misadventure he had missed during his absence. He kissed them in apology for the time he'd lost and in appreciation of the woman she'd become.

He would never take back their frenzied first encounter since his return, but it had been devoid of his favorite parts of lovemaking. He wanted to see all of her, feel all of her. He wanted to taste the ticklish skin behind her knees and breathe in the earthy fragrance of that incredible hair. He wanted to linger in everything just as much as his body argued for immediate release.

When his mouth found the most delicate part of her, he knew he'd have to keep her from writhing away from him. She had always lost control of herself when he did that, her skin burning hot. He secured his big hands over her hips and kept her still as he enjoyed the taste of her, lapping at her very essence.

She reached down to tug at his hair, her fingers warm and urgent against his scalp. She was stifling her cries into the silk-lined pillows on the bed, begging him to take her now as she rocked against the motion of his tongue.

There would be more time to savor her later, he told himself. They had the rest of their lives. Far be it for him to disregard a plea for the very thing every instinct was telling him he needed as well. He reared up, catching her mouth with his own, silencing her words with his tongue, and drove himself into her to the hilt.

She bit down on his lip, her nails scraping along the muscles of his back. She no longer clawed him to bleeding the way she had the first time they'd made love, all those years ago, but she had never been able to control pawing at him like a lioness while he took her in this way.

She wrapped her legs around his hips, linking her ankles as she bucked against him, holding herself close to him, unwilling to give up the taste of his lips even for the pleasure of their joining. She was no passive miss to be enjoyed, and never had been. She met him thrust for thrust, finding her own pleasure with a ragged cry that he drank down like ambrosia.

She slid her hands up along his neck, through his hair and onto either side of his face, her eyes sliding open as her body melted into satisfied bliss. "Callum," she breathed. "Mine."

"Yours," he agreed, his voice strained, body taut as his own pleasure rose within him. He remembered at the last moment what she had requested of him, almost a breath too late, and withdrew just in time to milk his final pleasure onto the softness of her thighs.

It was so overpowering, so completely satisfying, that he felt the will drain from his limbs, his strength depleted, his hunger sated. He collapsed onto her, ragged breaths coming in heavy gulps. Their thighs mingled, the slick result of their coupling smearing between their flesh.

He rolled onto his side, pulling her close to him. His eyelids were heavy, his body thoroughly taxed. Just for a moment, he thought, they could rest in each other's arms. Just for a moment, they could catch their breath. They could be at peace.

―――

He did not know how long he had dozed on the cusp of oblivion, but when he blinked back into the world, he found she had arrived ahead of him. Her eyes were already open and emerald bright, fixed upon his own. He reached down to slide his thumb across the curve of her cheek, marveling at the fact that she was here, tucked into his arms again.

She had come to him. She had come with the express intention of falling into his bed. It was more than he deserved to even hope for.

Chapter 16

What was it she had said? She had taken precautions? Against what?

"What did you mean," he whispered, twining his fingers into her curls, "when you said you took precautions?"

"Oh." She bit her lip, looking a little bashful. "Something I learned as a midwife, to prevent conception."

He blinked, the haze that had settled over his mind in the midst of desire clearing immediately. "But in the clinic ..."

"I am certain we didn't conceive in the clinic," she whispered, touching his hair. "But the risk we took was foolhardy."

He exhaled slowly, considering what she was saying. "That whole summer, we never even considered it. You might have very well ended up like Abigail Collins."

She was silent for a moment, still, with her eyes searching his face. "What if I had?" she finally whispered. "Then or now?"

He considered it, what it would have meant for them. In truth, he was not at all displeased with the idea of her growing round with his child. The thought sprouted in his mind with an idyllic light as he stroked her back. He could picture her with her hair down her back, large with her pregnancy, greeting him with a kiss in a field of heather which grew in the plains before a country homestead. It was something he realized he did want, very much, and soon it would be a real possibility. Their suffering had finally put him in a position to make it real.

"You would make a wonderful mother, Hel, but you are right that it's best we wait. Such a surprise would only mean that I must speak to your brother sooner than I had planned," he told her, "before everything was in place."

"My brother?" she repeated, her whisper replaced by a bewildered indignation. "What do my brothers have to do with anything?"

He chuckled, wanting nothing more than to kiss her until she understood him. "I wanted to wait, at least until I had purchased a property and a few mounts, enough to prove I can provide for us. I thought perhaps to breed carriage horses."

She pulled back, her brow wrinkled as she gazed up at him. "Again, what part do either of my brothers play in such thoughts?"

"Well," he said, smiling, "it is customary, is it not, to ask for the blessing of the head of a household if you wish to wed its daughter?"

"The head of House Somers is currently me, is it not?" she snapped. "Else you might consider that I have lived in the dower house these past years, not at Somerton. If you want someone's permission, you'd best ask my mother, then, as you do not wish for me simply to decide myself."

"Hel." He sighed, his exasperation tinted with affection. "I only wish to do this correctly, to be worthy of you."

"Yes, you've said before," she replied, collapsing back against his chest. "You always were, though, and I never wanted the proper way of things anyhow."

"I know," he replied. He pressed a kiss into the top of her head, relieved that she was not pulling away anymore. "I know."

"Stables," she pondered on a yawn. "It is not a bad thought. You've a way with horses."

"Heloise?" he said, his heart fit to melt within his chest. "Do you wish to marry me?"

"Mm," she replied, already dozing off again. "It is a lovely thought."

17

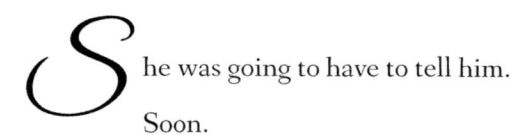

She was going to have to tell him.

Soon.

She still had no idea how to go about it. How does one tell a man such a thing?

Warm and sated, curled into bed with her, he had seemed pleased with the idea of putting a child in her. That's all it had been, though, an idea, a fantasy in which he pictured a baby from concept to birth, not a three-year-old girl who already spoke her thoughts and walked alone.

He had missed so very much. She had been driven by her anger about it, the knowledge of what he'd forced her to do alone, the resentment of what she'd lost. She had unquestioningly been the injured party in their affair, but now ... now she realized that he would never be able to reclaim some of the most precious moments of one's life.

He would never stand by awaiting his first child's birth. He would never hear her speak her first words or stand upright

Chapter 17

for the first time. He would never feel the kicks through a belly and anticipate all the possibilities of the future: boy or girl, green eyes or black, jolly or determined.

Callie was already a fully formed human, at a stage in life that was wholly honest. Childhood was when you were most untethered to artifice, most true to your inner self, before you learned how unacceptable you truly were.

Since the night she'd gone to his room, every one of those silly little notes he still insisted on sending her had brought with it both a flush of pleasure and a twinge of guilt. The flowers she pressed into the book he'd sent her all those years ago, so that one day perhaps their daughter could have them, if he did not choose to stay once he knew of her existence.

She pushed the food around on her plate with the back of her fork, frowning down at a perfectly appetizing dinner as her thoughts consumed her. Her mother had insisted on a family dinner at the dower house tonight, so that they didn't entirely lose touch with normalcy.

Rose and Gideon had sent word that they were about a day's ride away, staying at an inn in the town where they'd gotten married. Rose's progressing condition had rendered her a sight more fatigued than she might otherwise be, but they promised to return within the week. Like the Blakelys, they had been gone for far longer than anyone had anticipated. Such was the way of traveling this far north in the winter.

"I'm surprised Reverend Halliwell isn't here tonight," Alex commented, a taunting sparkle in his eyes. "He certainly has been a regular staple in your orbit, Mother."

"Tonight is a *family* dinner, my love," his wife reminded him, placing a gloved hand on his arm.

Alex scoffed. "Then why is Sheldon here?"

Sheldon Bywater's head snapped up, his expression deeply affronted. He jabbed the drumstick he had been eating in Alex's direction. "I've been a part of this family longer than you have, boy."

"It's true," Ruthie confirmed, motioning to have more wine added to her glass. "He spent more of his childhood here than at Moorvale."

Alex was not satisfied, his gaze still keen and shrewd on their mother. Not having gotten the reaction he wanted, he opted for a more direct attack. "At this rate, I wouldn't be surprised if the reverend's title changed to Step-Father Halliwell in short enough order ... or isn't that your intention?"

"Alex!" both Gloriana and Heloise hissed in unison, only broadening his grin.

Ruthie sighed, taking a deep drink of her wine and then setting the crystal glass back onto the tablecloth with as much dignity as she could muster. "Is there something you wish to ask me, Alexander?"

"I believe I've already asked it, in so many words," he replied cheerily, snatching up his own wine glass as he awaited the results of his prodding.

Heloise turned to her mother, admittedly curious. Sometimes Alex's complete lack of tact resulted in some rather satisfying information.

Chapter 17

Was she imagining it, or had her mother stopped applying chestnut dye to her hair? In this light it looked as though gleaming strands of silver were beginning to show through, winding their way around her ringlets. It became her rather well, Hel thought.

"Yes, all right. The reverend has asked me to marry him," Ruthie said, as though it were the most casual information in the world. "I have tentatively accepted, so long as we can come to an accord on some of the finer details of the arrangement. I did not plan to make an announcement until your brother was returned and all the odds and ends had been stamped out."

Heloise turned wide-eyed to her brother, who tossed her a wink.

"What details?" Sheldon asked curiously. "Isn't the whole process rather straightforward?"

"One might note that you've yet to go through it yourself, Lord Moorvale," Gloriana said fondly, "and perhaps as such are innocent to its nuances."

"Just so," Ruthie agreed with a little shrug. "He expects me to move into that tiny parish house, which is absurd when my dower house is already outfitted and functioning and far more spacious. I said as much, but he is aghast at the idea of living here with me, and so we are currently at an impasse."

"Mother, you can't move a new husband into the dower house," Heloise said patiently. "Gideon would have heart failure at the sheer scandal of it."

"Oh, I can do whatever I like," Ruthie snapped back. "I'm rich, aren't I?"

"You are," Alex agreed, "which is why I can't figure out what you hope to gain from marrying Halliwell. You'll lose your title and your status, inspiring no jealousy in anyone at all. It is like I barely know you."

"I can't think what you mean," Ruthie replied coldly.

"Mm," Alex commented, shaking his head with that typical incendiary smile. "I'm certain you can."

Ruthie watched him through narrowed eyes as he returned to his meal with gusto, next to an aghast Gloriana. "It was Polly," she finally confessed, bringing his attention back to her.

"My mother?" Gloriana asked, confusion evident on her face.

"Yes, darling," Ruthie said without looking away from Alex. "Do you remember what I told you, Alex, on the night I gave you that ring that your bride now wears?"

"I do," he replied, some of the smugness melting from his face.

"It was a good reminder," Ruthie said. "She encouraged me to consider, if I married again, taking the path she had chosen rather than the one I'd already traveled. That is what I am doing, my son, as you did."

"For those of us not present for that conversation," Heloise put in, irritated by the sudden tense silence between her brother and mother, "perhaps you'd care to elaborate?"

"She likes him," Alex provided, turning to her wide-eyed. "She actually just really enjoys his company."

"As good a reason as any," Sheldon commented, startling

everyone at the reminder that he was still there, eating his dinner, as though nothing at all was amiss.

---

*J*t was later, as the same group enjoyed the warmth of the drawing room fire, that Alex, in his way, apologized to their mother.

"I should not have assumed the worst," he said, squeezing her hand as he knelt at her feet. "You will make a beautiful bride."

"Yes, fine," Ruthie tutted, pulling her hand away to pat his cheek. "Pour us a drink and we shall toast to better days ahead."

Next to Heloise on the settee, Gloriana gave a little sigh of relief, her eyes following her husband as he filled two tumblers from an ornate display by the fireplace.

Hel turned to her with amusement, scratching absently at Echo's ears as the dog stretched her limbs on the softness of the couch cushions. "I hope you are still going to scold him," she said.

"Oh, yes," Glory confirmed with a nod, "but now it need merely be a ceremonial scolding."

Sheldon was watching the two of them with a grim expression on his face. Echo seemed to catch wind of this disapproval, turning her warm, brown eyes in his direction and giving a whimper, but otherwise making no movement toward returning to his side.

His brows beetled together, eyes locked on his beloved companion.

Heloise hid her smile. She had noticed the bloodhound's uncharacteristic laziness about a week ago, and at first had also been concerned. She cooed to Echo, urging the dog to show her belly for a good rubbing, and confirmed again that what ailed Echo was nothing dire, after all.

"She hasn't been herself," Sheldon grumbled, attempting to disguise concern with discontent. "She sleeps all day and has no interest in a hard day's work."

"Women rarely wish to exert themselves when they're expecting," Heloise replied easily, raising her eyes to watch the shock wind its way through him. "Congratulations, Moorvale, you're going to be a grandfather."

"What!" he barked, coming to his feet, which only made his dog whine again. "How? When!"

"The night of the fire, I suspect," Heloise responded, aware that all eyes had been drawn to this poor, compromised dog in her lap. "You did put her in the kennels with the other dogs. Perhaps she found one she likes."

He blinked, his mouth opening and closing in an attempt to reply, and instead just settled back into his seat. "What am I going to do with a litter of mutts?" he mumbled, passing a hand over his face. "What was she thinking?"

"The choices of parents are hardly the fault of their children," Heloise sniffed. "It isn't for you to assume the puppies will be worthless."

"They won't be purebred," he retorted. "They'll be mongrels."

Chapter 17

"And I suppose that makes them undeserving?" Heloise snapped. "Perhaps Echo mated with a strong hunting dog or a shrewd tracker. Their progeny may have value you've not yet considered, and be worthy of their own merit."

"No one wants mutts!" he insisted stubbornly. "I don't see why you lot ought to take it personally."

"I will have one," Gloriana put in. "You did once promise me a puppy of my own, and I should love a mutt just as much as any other."

Sheldon looked baffled, turning his head toward the other woman. "But why would you want a mutt when you could have your pick of tested breeds, certain to be suited to your desires?"

"Perhaps because bloodlines do not necessarily determine our value nor our compatibility," Heloise replied sharply. "And if you love Echo, you will love her young."

Alex rubbed his hand over his mouth, obviously attempting to suppress laughter, while Sheldon looked from woman to woman with pure befuddlement.

"It was her choice," Heloise persisted, fire in her voice. "You might expect it was a good one."

"Fine!" he grumbled, crossing his arms across his chest. "She just ought to have consulted me first, is all. I only want what's best for her."

"Oh Sheldon, my dear boy," Ruthie chuckled. "You have much to learn about women."

18

Callum couldn't resist checking his reflection every few seconds and attempting one last time to make himself presentable to a peer. Of course, every time he turned to look into the mirror hung on the drawing room wall, he found another hair out of place, another speck on his coat. It was only making him more nervous.

If you want someone's permission, she'd said, *you'd best ask my mother.*

The parlor maid who'd shown him in had assured him that the dowager viscountess would be returned shortly if he wouldn't mind waiting. He wondered now if he ought to have just come back at a later time.

The thought occurred to him too late, of course. He could hear voices now, one of which was markedly Yankee and speaking with the authority of a woman who has never been questioned. He straightened his posture just in time as the door was pushed open by Ruthie Somers herself, trailed by scandalized maids who she tossed her gloves to as she spoke.

"Have the chocolate sent up immediately so that it has time to cool," she told them, reaching to her throat to unclasp the cloak she wore. "Once they're dry and dressed, bring them back down here. We will enjoy the fire together."

"Yes, My Lady," both maids murmured, backing out of the room with quick glances darted at one another.

"Ah, Lieutenant!" Ruthie said, clasping her hands together, her cheeks bright with color. "What wonderful timing. You must stay for hot chocolate and tea cakes. The children will join us momentarily. We've just been enjoying some of the fresh snowfall together out of doors, though between you and me, warming up is the part I always look forward to the most."

He hesitated, overwhelmed by the way she pelted other people with her rapid-fire words. "I wished to discuss a matter of some importance with you," he said, perhaps a little lamely.

"Yes, of course." She motioned to the couch opposite the fire, sweeping into a seated position on its far end without awaiting his acceptance. "I imagine you are here to report on the rehousing. How is it coming along? I hope my absence is not a hindrance, but you understand one has other duties to attend when running a household."

"It is going well," he said, perching himself on the cushion farthest from Lady Somers. "The patchwork was done on the houses that could manage with simple repair, and the church is far less crowded now that some people are able to return home."

"Mm," Ruthie said, motioning for staff to bring in the trays for teatime. "I expect Mrs. Collins in particular was beside herself with relief that her daughter would have at least a few days of proper confinement."

"They were returned home as our first priority," he confirmed. "Lady Heloise insisted."

"Naturally," Ruthie responded with a little quirk of her lips.

They fell into silence as sweetened hot chocolate was poured into two mugs for the adults and two small cups with spout attachments for the children, both left open to cool, curls of fragrant steam rising from their centers.

Callum wasn't sure if it was simply for want of distraction, but the first taste of the chocolate did seem to fortify him, calming some of the anxious buzzing that had begun roundabouts his midsection. He took a deep drink as two very young children were ushered in by their nannies, a boy and a girl, neither more than a handful of years old.

"Ah," Ruthie said happily, holding her hand out. "Come meet the lieutenant, children."

Only the boy came forward, the other shying behind her nanny's skirts and hiding her face in them.

"Oh, Caroline," Ruthie said unhappily. "You must learn to be a brave girl. You promised to try!"

The child gave a muffled response that sounded something like, "Sorry, Granny," but made no move to depart the safety of the starched skirts she had folded around herself. The other one, the boy, had blown right past his grandmother and up to Callum's knee, which he gripped in his tiny hands as he peered up into this stranger's face.

Chapter 18

"Reggie," Ruthie said patiently. "This is Lieutenant Laughlin. He is a soldier!"

The child's large, golden eyes widened, his thick lashes blinking rapidly as he examined Callum's face. "Stay," he commanded, then turned over his shoulder to peer at the tray. "Chocolate?"

"Yes, chocolate and then a nap," Ruthie told him. "Just as I said before."

The child drew his lips down in an exaggerated frown, whipping his hand out and knocking over one of the small cups, which flooded the tray with liquid chocolate. "No nap!" he announced.

"Master Reggie!" his nanny scolded, rushing forward to attempt to mitigate the mess. "That was very naughty!"

He turned those furious eyes up to Callum, as though he were looking for an ally in this war, and whispered loudly, "Hate naps!"

"Yes, well, life is very difficult for us all, Reggie. Now you have to wait for your chocolate to cool down again because you spilled it," Ruthie tutted. "Go sit by the window and wait until I call you."

"Come along, Master Reggie," the other nanny coaxed, holding her hand out to be grabbed by the willful little boy as he jerked her with a rather surprising amount of gusto toward his punishment spot.

Callum watched him go with a sort of impressed shock. "That is the viscount's son?" he asked, just to be certain.

Ruthie gave a beleaguered sigh. "That's what I was told, but I'm just as skeptical as you are. If he weren't the spit of a Somers, I'd have Rose interrogated on the matter of his origins."

Callum coughed, some of the chocolate he was sipping finding its way into the wrong portion of his throat at such a statement.

The other child was standing with her head down, her ringlets covering her face and glimmering with red strands against a darker base, dutifully awaiting her cup of chocolate. He noticed that she had a rag dolly tucked into her side. It was not the fine dolls one usually bestowed on children of status, but instead a well-loved, stain-speckled craft of common goods that the girl seemed to clutch by habit.

"Yes," Ruthie said as though she could read his thoughts, "Callie is much easier."

"Callie," he repeated, his eyes on the shy little girl. "Why, we almost have the same name, little one."

She seemed to take a deep breath, perhaps building up enough bravery to face an interloper, and turned over her shoulder to look at him. "What is your name?" she asked in a feather-soft voice.

"It's Callum," he replied, in the instant before the wind was knocked from his body. He was frozen into place, his skin prickling with a deep, eerie recognition as she turned that little face toward him.

He knew that face. He'd know it anywhere.

He forced himself to set his mug down before his hands

began to shake and crossed to the other side of the table. He lowered himself to his knees, opposite the little girl, who blinked shyly but did not cower from him. "How old are you, Callie?" he managed, though his throat was very dry and he knew what the answer must be.

"Three," she whispered back, seemingly relieved that he had come close enough that she need not project her voice, "and a half."

"No need to rush to age four, young lady," Ruthie responded jovially.

The little girl blushed at this correction, turning her eyes up to meet Callum's by way of apology. Her irises were a brown so dark that it was nearly black, blending into the darkness of her pupils so well that he knew, in her later years, that some people would find it unsettling. Those were his mother's eyes. Those were *his* eyes.

He reached out with trembling hands and touched the side of her face, hot tears welling up in his own eyes. He traced her plump little cheek down to the sharp point of her chin. How was this possible?

It was only then that Ruthie seemed to become aware that this was not a simple introduction between child and adult. She sucked in her breath, the ceramic of her mug clattering into its saucer, but did not otherwise move or speak.

He ran his fingers down the soft lines of the little girl's arm, and held her delicate hand in his own. She looked back wide-eyed, but did not resist this touch. Instead, she reached forward and brushed the tear off his cheek with her other hand, and whispered softly, "It's okay. Don't cry."

He laughed. Or sobbed. The sound was somewhere in between the two. He wanted to pull her into his arms and hold her tight to his chest, but he did not wish to frighten her.

He turned back to Ruthie, blinking loose another set of tears down his cheeks, and found her stricken, staring at the two of them with enough shock on her face that he felt certain she hadn't made the connection either, until just this moment.

"I didn't know," he rasped, squeezing his eyes shut. "I never knew."

In his mind's eye, he saw those silver scars on Heloise's hip that he'd traced so casually. He knew what they were now. No accident had caused them. Such were the marks a woman gets as her belly swells with child, her skin straining to accommodate the miracle of life.

What was it he had said to her a few nights prior?

You might have ended up like Abigail Collins.

It was a wonder she hadn't slapped him across the face at that. It was a wonder she would even look at him still. She had been holding this secret against her heart all this time, alone.

"Millie," Ruthie said to the boy's nanny. "Please take Master Reggie up to the nursery. Anne, you will accompany them. I will tuck our Caroline in myself when she is ready for her nap."

Both girls bobbed immediate curtsies, hastening to obey this order, both keeping their eyes downcast. Before they could reach the door to the drawing room, Ruthie added in a voice that was deceptively cool and calm, "I expect you both understand that gossiping is not tolerated in this house."

They both nodded, scurrying out, shushing the indignant arguments of the little lord and allowing the door to snap firmly shut behind them.

Through it all, Callie had stayed still, gazing at Callum with curiosity and clinging to his hand. She pushed her little rag doll forward, onto his knee.

"She helps," the little girl said to him, stroking the doll's rag-crafted hair. "You can borrow her."

"Thank you, Caroline," he whispered back, holding the little doll to his chest the way he wished he could hold her. "I already feel better."

She smiled then, dimples in her cheeks and a sparkle in her eyes, brightening against her bashful nature. She looked so very pleased to have been of assistance, and reached forward once more to clear the tears from his cheeks with the flat of her hand.

He knew it must be confusing for a child, such a little thing, to see an adult crying and smiling at the same time, especially some strange man, doing it by way of an introduction. What else could he do, though? It was too much to learn all at once. The sight of her had filled him with a brimming of so much emotion, he didn't think he could stand it.

Flashes of so many things collided within him. If he didn't have such a will to remain knelt on the carpet, gazing into her face, soaking in everything about her, committing her to memory, he very well might have passed out from the shock of it.

"Why don't you both come sit," Ruthie suggested softly, a tell-tale glimmer of moisture reflecting in her own eyes. "It appears your acquaintance is long overdue."

Somehow, he had arrived at tea time and stayed until supper, which Ruthie insisted be served in the drawing room, where he'd passed the last several hours.

Getting to know a three-year-old, it turned out, was a sight more complex than his usual social challenges. It wasn't until little Caroline had been prompted by her grandmother to describe the snowman she had built earlier today that her cloak of shyness seemed to slip away.

She had told him her favorite color (yellow), her favorite food (jam on toast), and that she was learning to count (only to ten, though). She had stopped speaking several times to smile and touch his face again, asking more than once, "All better?"

She had been fascinated with him, the way children are with any new novelty, and had chosen to sit upon his lap while they chatted, observed by a mostly silent, possibly weeping Ruthie Somers.

"She picked up the numbers very quickly," Ruthie had interjected, pride apparent in her voice when that particular tidbit had been mentioned. "Any Cunningham worth her salt has a natural talent for sums."

Chapter 18

"Cunningham," he'd repeated, glancing over at the dowager. "Is that the name she was given?"

Ruthie had hesitated, looking immediately caught in a snare of discomfort. "She is meant to be a distant relation that I brought with me from Philadelphia," she said apologetically. "We couldn't rightly call her a Somers."

"Or a Laughlin," he'd agreed with a solemn nod. He looked down at the curious eyes of his child, who did not bear his name. "Does my mother know?"

"If she does, she's never breathed a word of it," Ruthie answered. "I don't think Heloise has told anyone, ever."

He was drawn back into conversation about far more important things by his daughter, and did not revisit such boring, adult topics until Callie had begun to lightly snore, her head pressed against his chest, and her hand resting on the doll he still held. The warmth of her little body, limp in sleep, the trust in her even breathing made him want to weep in earnest.

"Tell me how it was," he asked quietly, staring into the fire instead of confronting the woman next to him. "I will ask her, but I don't know that she'll tell me the whole of it. I don't know that she was ever intending to tell me *any* of it."

There was a beat of silence between them as the past hovered heavily over the room.

"She fled her boarding school for Somerton at the break of spring that year," Ruthie said, "once she could no longer hide her condition. I didn't arrive for over two months after that, for receiving her letter across the ocean and then putting myself right back across is not a rapid thing. By the time I'd returned home, she was almost ready to give birth and seemed well settled into her plight. All I could offer was a feasible story so that we might keep the baby, when she arrived."

He shuddered, chilled by the thought of his child being bundled up and sent to an orphanage. What would they have done with her, if the dowager had not returned?

"Gideon was willing to claim the baby as his bastard, should it be a boy," Ruthie said, anticipating his next question. "For a girl, things are more complex. There is no place in the world for a girl born on the wrong side of the blanket. Even a life in service would have been a challenge."

He squeezed his eyes shut. What had he been doing at the time of her birth? What frivolous complaint had he been nursing about his status in the world and his discomfort in the barracks? All the while ...

"No one caught wind of her pregnancy," Ruthie said, her voice a flat cadence in the silent foreboding of the room. She spoke as though her explanations would ease the pain that radiated off him, and perhaps silence her own guilt. "She has always been tempestuous, so running away from school and refusing a debut surprised no one who knew her. The scandal of her apparent choices was far preferable to the truth. Caroline calls her Auntie. We were to tell her the truth once she was old enough to understand it."

"I had come here today to speak about Heloise," he confessed, too spent emotionally to remember his anxiety, too tired to turn his head from the comforting chaos of the flames in the hearth. "I was going to ask for your blessing to marry her, if she'd have me. I have been a fool."

Chapter 18

"I should have known," Ruthie murmured, a note of misery in her voice. "I should have put it together. It seems so obvious now."

"If you didn't, that means no one else did either," he said flatly. "So, it is just as well."

"All the same," she whispered. "I hope you make a more attentive parent than I. This is not the first time that I have failed my daughter."

The chime and slam of the main entrance startled them both, though the jerk of Callum's body only made Callie readjust her posture, snuggling into his chest with a contented sigh. Both Callum and Ruthie had frozen, though of course they must have both known in the back of their minds that she would eventually return home.

"Mother?" called Heloise through the door as she stomped the snow off her boots in the entryway. "I've had the most wonderful day. It is the first time since the fire that I've truly believed that the township will make a full recovery."

She went quiet for a moment, likely removing her cloak and putting her feet into a pair of dry slippers. Her footsteps drew nearer, her voice still raised as she made her way to the drawing room. "Gideon brought home so many things that have made all the difference," she said, her face bright and merry as she pushed the door open. "I'm only hoping to …"

She trailed off, her eyes locking onto her child in the arms of that child's father. The color in her cheeks drained away, her hand tightening into a fist around the knob of the door. She looked the way he had felt some hours prior.

She took several fortifying breaths, the silence in the room playing host to the sound of her inhalations. "Callum," she began, though she made no move to come closer, her body leaning against the frame of the door as though it were the only thing keeping her upright.

"Heloise," he answered, his voice even and steady, revealing nothing. He did not want to play this the wrong way. He didn't want to lose them both, forever.

A frantic pounding on the front door stopped her from whatever speech she might have launched into, her startled posture leaning heavily against the support of the door. "Oh, what now!" she breathed, turning on her heel and pacing out of view.

From their seats, they could hear the howling of the wind as she pried the door open, and the silence that followed it slamming shut again. The voice of the intruder was a frantic one, high-pitched and afraid.

"Lady Heloise, you must come right away," it said.

"I cannot," Heloise attempted to respond, though she barely got the words out.

"You must! Miss Abigail has taken an awful fall and now ... there's blood and ... and water. She hit her head. You must come!"

Heloise hissed in frustration, still out of view, though the weight of her choices fell heavy on those who could hear. "Saddle my horse," she said to the frantic voice. "I will be right out."

She appeared in the doorway again, alight with purpose and panic. She looked angelic, he thought, in the way that angels had once fought great wars against forces of evil. "I am sorry, but I must go," she breathed, her eyes darting between her mother and Callum. "I must."

"Go," he replied. "I will be waiting."

She nodded, setting her jaw against the implications of that, and just as suddenly as she appeared, Heloise Somers was gone again.

19

Another crisis was a blessing, in its own way. What better distraction was there from deep, paralyzing panic than something so dire that one cannot, in good conscience, think of anything else?

Abigail had slipped on the ice outside of the cottage while attempting to bring the laborers some of her mother's freshly baked bread. For all the many preparations they had made for the homes that could be re-inhabited, somehow everyone involved had neglected to clear the rear pathways that connected house to house. It had been a stupid oversight, one that Heloise would never forgive herself for, especially if this accident ended in tragedy.

She arrived at the cottage to find three men hovering worriedly near a basket of overturned, frozen bread and streaks of blood on the ice. They fell into step with her as she approached the house.

The one who had fetched her from the dower house, the

Chapter 19

youngest of them, said, "Please tell us if there's anything you need, My Lady."

Abby had a lump on her head and was dazed, but at the instruction of Mrs. Collins, the men had carried her inside and laid her back into the bed. She lulled in and out of consciousness, blinking at Heloise with a dazed smile of confusion or perhaps relief.

"Fetch Dr. Garber," Hel had instructed one of the laborers. "Tell him what has happened."

To the others, she asked to stable Boudicea and bring firewood to keep the cottage warm.

She busied herself preparing the room for a birth, taking care to ensure that Abigail remained lucid. There was little else she could do. With the womb water breached by the fall, there was no stopping the arrival of the baby now. She did not wish pain on any of her charges, but tonight she prayed for the contractions to begin, for the shock of them might pull Abby from her addled state.

When the handful of raspberry leaves she'd retrieved from her kit and thrown into boiling water had sufficiently steeped, she scooped up a handful of snow from the windowsill and dropped it into the cup. She climbed into the bed next to Abby, supporting her upright, as she held the lukewarm liquid to her lips and murmured encouragement to drink it all down.

She left her only when she could answer simple questions, slipping her back onto her pillows and returning her feet to the uneven wooden floor to resume her work. She opened the window again and packed more snow into a thin pouch made from a sheep's bladder. She placed it on the lump that had formed on Abigail's forehead, instructing Mrs. Collins to hold it in place as she busied herself around the cottage, preparing for the inevitable.

"Keep her awake," she instructed. "Talk to her, engage her. She must not fall asleep."

Her preference was to manage birthing on a chair, so that the aid of gravity and the necessity of staying upright both assisted the mother with the difficult task ahead of her. However, with this particular mother currently dazed from her fall, she did not wish to risk it. The babe, by the mercy of God, seemed well, despite the abrupt nature of the onset of labor.

The child's body was fully turned and ready to descend, and the blood that had been present from the rupture of Abigail's water had been perfectly normal, though she was certain this information had been cold comfort to the men who'd found her and lingered at the house until Heloise arrived.

The first cry of pain that ripped from Abigail's throat flooded Hel with so much relief that she thought she might burst into tears. Upon inspection, the dilation process had begun, though barely, and nothing yet seemed amiss with the arrival of this child. Still, just to be safe, she applied the primrose oil from her midwifery kit and massaged the stomach the way Meggie had taught her to when labor must be induced or otherwise encouraged. She wanted to take no chances.

Beyond the bump on her head, Abigail had skinned the

flesh from her elbow and bruised one of her thighs rather badly. Aside from some slapdash bandaging, Heloise could not spare the attention to those injuries, and hoped that they were minor. She could not give laudanum or willow bark to Abigail for fear of thinning her blood, and instead simply refreshed the presence of snow against the wounds as she waited for the doctor's arrival.

It was a blissful buzz of necessity that drowned out the bone-chilling shock she'd had upon walking into that drawing room. She blinked to dispel the memory of it, forcing herself to put her mind into the present moment. To do anything else would be akin to cracking the lid on Pandora's box, and she simply could not afford to do so until her work here had been completed.

She kept an ear turned to Abigail and her mother, talking in low voices of frivolity and memories and plans for the future as she gathered towels and linens and rags to assist in the things still yet to come.

She flew to the door the instant she heard a rap upon it, and pried it open, expecting to find Richard Garber and his medical kit at the ready. Instead it was only that weary laborer she'd sent on the errand. "Where is the doctor?" she demanded.

"He won't come," the man responded, shuffling his feet in obvious discomfort. "He says it ain't proper."

Heloise blinked at the man, too stunned by the stupidity of that statement to reply, and by the time her wits had returned to her, he had already gone. She stood in the doorway, getting coated with the lazy drift of snow, with no choices but to go retrieve the man herself or to make do without him.

She made herself shut the door, dust off her skirts, and walk back to the bed, her face likely drawn with discontent. It wasn't until she saw both Abigail and her mother that she realized their talking had stopped completely, and both were staring at her, their hands clasped together.

"He wouldn't come, would he?" Abigail said softly, in a way that wasn't really a question. "I thought when the moment arrived, he might finally come, but he won't. He's not coming."

"Perhaps once the babe arrives," Mrs. Collins offered, with no real conviction in her voice, as Abigail began to cry.

"No, he won't," she argued, her voice cracking. "He hasn't so much as looked at me since I found out, and the one time I attempted to confront him ... well, you know what happened, Mama."

"What happened?" Heloise asked, careful to keep her voice gentle and without judgement. She crossed the room and sat on the side of the bed opposite Mrs. Collins, taking Abigail's other hand. "What did he do?"

"Nothing," Abigail said miserably, a deep sob racking her body. "It was all my fault, and if I tell you, you're like to tell the constable and they'll take my baby away."

Heloise raised her eyes, bewildered, to Mrs. Collins, who simply shook her head and averted her eyes, unwilling to reveal anything that her daughter didn't wish to be known. She stroked the short, brown tresses of Abigail's hair, allowing her to cry as much as she needed to. Lord knew she wished she could cry like that too, just now.

The next contraction interrupted her misery with a sharp gasp of pain, her eyes flying open in surprise as her knees came up from the bed. When it released her, she seemed to have regained some sense of control, though perhaps trading one pain for another was not the best way for such things to happen.

"I won't let anyone take your baby away from you," Heloise said to her. "You have my word. No matter what has happened."

Abigail shook her head, reaching forward for the sheet to press the tears from her eyes. "You'll hate me."

Heloise hesitated, her heart pounding in her chest with indignation and anger and fear and sadness. She knew she ought not say a single word, especially with how delicate the situation currently sat back at Somerton, but instead she reached forward to tip Abigail's face toward her, looking hard into those sweet, brown eyes. "Abby," she said. "I have a child too."

She ignored the gasp from Mrs. Collins and the way the older woman's hands flew up to cover her mouth. She didn't care anymore. Why should she enjoy the shroud of protection from her family when Abigail had done nothing more than she had, and was shunned? They were the same, were they not? Victims of their own desire and the plight of women in an unjust world.

"Her father was not there while I was expecting either," she continued. "I understand. I truly do."

"The little American girl," Abigail whispered after a moment. "She is yours?"

Heloise nodded, her skin erupting in gooseflesh. She wasn't certain what the feeling that cracked open within her was at sharing this secret, but in that fraught moment, she might have called it relief.

Abigail reached for Heloise's wrist and turned her face to place a kiss into the palm of her hand. It was such a sweet gesture, so genuine and affectionate, that Heloise knew her secret would be kept. She gently lowered their linked hands onto the bed, but turned her face away again, as though what she must say next was too painful to reveal with Heloise's eyes on her face.

"The day of your brother's wedding, you came to me and told me the babe had moved, climbed into position, and was ready to appear any day now," she began, stopping to swallow down the trembling in her voice. "It was the first time I had thought of this pregnancy as a real, true baby, about to enter the world and be all the things a person is. I was so excited and I thought that perhaps that realization, that frame of thinking, might have been the only thing missing for Richard. I thought surely if he heard what you'd said, he'd realize that our baby was a real person and he would wish to be a real father."

Heloise squeezed her hand, but did not otherwise respond.

"I went to the clinic and waited for him. He often goes there at night to be about his work in the quiet, to write his logs for the day. Before I got with child, I used to sit with him and help and we were happy, so I thought maybe in that place, we could be happy again.

Chapter 19

"So, I lit some tapers by the window and waited and waited and waited. It kept getting colder and darker and he never came. I don't know how long it took me to realize that it was the night of the new year. Locked up in this house, I'd lost all sense of time, but I could hear the revels and the singing and came to the realization that he likely was at the inn or at the manor, merry and warm and celebrating, without a second thought for me or our child." She shook her head, squeezing her eyes shut. "I was so upset. I gathered my skirts and ran home and crawled into bed, crying myself into a stupor until sleep took me.

"I left those candles burning, Lady Heloise. I left them so close to the herbs and the curtains and the wooden walls. It was my fault the township burned."

The silence hung heavy around them, the weight of what she'd just said settling over the room, just as heavy as the veil of smoke had been on the night of the fire. They seemed frozen in the wake of her revelation until another cry of pain forced the shock from all three of them as Abigail's body curled upon itself through the torment.

Heloise stood, bustling to the foot of the bed to check again that all was as it should be. As ever, her work gave her something to do with her hands and eyes and mind other than whatever fresh horror was haunting her. Tonight she could simply prolong the necessity of reacting to the revelation that Abigail had very likely been the cause of the fire. Heloise knew that when a woman was heavy with child, she was often not at her sharpest of mind, often forgetful and muddled. Such a mistake could have easily been her own when she was pregnant with Callie.

She wasn't angry or outraged or scandalized. She didn't know what she was feeling.

What would Callum have done, if he had been at Somerton instead of off at war? Would he have immediately insisted upon marrying her? Would he have left it for her to decide? Would he have behaved like the good doctor and continued pursuing another, more suitable woman while ignoring the inconvenience of an unwanted child?

Memories of the flirtatious banter she had entertained with Richard Garber made her feel ill. Worse, perhaps, was the realization that she had never suspected him of duplicity. In another life, she might have genuinely considered his proposals for her hand and been flattered to do so. It was terrifying to realize how easily fooled she had been, trusting that gentleman would behave as his status demanded.

"All that has befallen you is his fault," she decided, raising her eyes to meet Abigail's. "I do not blame you and neither will anyone else. We will make this right, Abby, I promise you, but first, we need to birth this baby, who will be safe and whole and happy. All right? Everything will be well."

Abigail nodded, sucking in what sounded like another sob before it could escape her. If she didn't believe such optimism, she gave no indication of it. She simply leaned back on her pillows, allowing her mother to put the cold pack on her bruised head, and braced herself for the hours to come.

Together, the three women worked throughout the night to bring a new life into the world.

Chapter 19

The child arrived just after the sun rose, thrashing and indignant and perfectly healthy.

Such was the giddy relief that always followed a long labor that for a time, all that had transpired the night before was forgotten. Mother and child were well, despite the cries that had sounded from the both this morning, and the flood of relief that always followed a healthy birth was a far more potent sensation than any mortal worries that might have hovered over them beforehand.

It wasn't until she had tidied the room, bundled the soiled linens, and began to pack away her midwifery box that Heloise began to remember the things that had happened the previous evening. Her hands started to shake as she filed her herbs and oils into their rightful places, a glow of white-hot anger growing in her chest at an alarming rate.

She welcomed it, stoked the heat of it within her. As long as she was furious, she couldn't feel the other things that lingered on the fringes. Her rage drowned out the panic and worry and guilt that lay so dangerously close to the surface of her thoughts.

She checked one last time on the Collins family, and found all three generations curled into one another on that big bed, asleep. She took care in putting her cloak back on and gathering her things. She would return for the soiled linens later, when they had rested for a bit, and could listen to her instructions on the essential first days of the child's life.

She stepped out into the morning light and took a deep gasp of the crisp winter air. The sun had already begun to travel toward the apex of the sky, always in such a hurry this time of year, to appear and then vanish again as quickly as possible.

It wasn't until she was several steps from the cottage that she allowed her steps to become heavier, her breathing harder. She kicked up winter around her, her breath a fog of heat as flecks of ice exploded around her feet. She walked with speed and determination toward the church, where she knew most of the township would be gathered just now for porridge, as Garber did his morning rounds.

She wanted an audience. She wanted to leave Richard Garber no means of wriggling free of the confrontation she had simmering within her.

Why should women bear all of the pain and consequence alone? Why should Society forgive men for their transgressions? Furthermore, what kind of a monster turned his back on his own child? He had proposed to Heloise, so casually, the very same day that Abigail had thought to beseech his sense of decency, his humanity and inborn love, one last time.

The steeple that topped their little parish church rose over the other buildings as she drew nearer, the buzz of voices from behind its doors growing louder as the path fell away beneath her feet.

She made her entrance on a gust of frozen wind, using the weight of her body to shut the door behind her and blinking away the sudden change in light. Just as she'd anticipated, there was a long queue around the pews as people waited for their cup of porridge, served today by their recently returned viscountess herself.

Rose glowed with the joy of her own pregnancy, in the security and comfort of a safe and loving marriage. She felt no shame resting her hand on the swell beneath her gown, and accepted hearty congratulations from the very same people who would turn to the side should Abigail Collins pass by them these last months. Rose Somers felt no need to hide within the safety of her home, for fear that anyone might see and know her shame.

Hel's eyes fell on Dr. Garber, who stood apart from the innkeeper with the burned leg, absently scribbling in the little book of records he kept in his jacket. His brow was unlined with concern, his posture casual. He had been told last night about Abigail's fall, and that it had hastened her labor, and yet here he was, well-rested and at ease, seemingly completely indifferent to the status of either Abby herself or his infant child.

She affixed onto her face what must have been a terrible smile, tucking the box under her arm and throwing the hood on her cloak back. He caught sight of her as she drew within a few steps of him, his face reflecting a benign and oblivious pleasure to see her.

"Good morning, Lady Heloise," he said, snapping his little notebook shut and tucking it into his jacket.

"Good morning, Dr. Garber," she replied, a little louder than strictly necessary. "I am soon to return home for some rest, for it has been a long and difficult night, but I thought you'd like to know that you have a son."

He gave a nervous smile, though his eyes flashed with something like panic. "I beg your par—"

"He is healthy and his mother will recover from her fall in time," Heloise continued, raising her voice to drown him out. "Which you would know if you had attended us last night when requested."

The room had gone deadly silent. All the bustle of morning activity had ceased, a sea of curious eyes turned in their direction.

"You are mistaken," he replied, his posture frozen, eyes hard. "You have had a long night and are not yourself."

"I saw the child," Hel returned, her voice falling to an angry whisper. She need not shout now to be heard. "He is yours. If you had been present, you might have had a chance to name him, but as you were not, he is now called William, after the late Mr. Collins. I daresay a more noble namesake than he might otherwise have been saddled with."

Rose appeared at her elbow, laying a calming hand upon it, her face a mask of placidity. "It is such a shame," she said wanly, "that so many important things were lost in the blaze, Dr. Garber. I'm certain that you can have another marriage license delivered in short order, with a note in our records to assure future generations of little William's legitimacy."

"Absolutely right," Reverend Halliwell intoned from the rear of the room, starting Dr. Garber visibly. "We would expect nothing less from the man our township trusts with their very lives. After all, it was so very generous of you to remain at your duties rather than whisking Miss Collins off to Scotland before she could give birth."

Garber took a step forward, attempting to speak so low that he could not be overheard. "We took precautions. There must have been someone else."

"Richard," Heloise snipped. "If you did not drop into a dead faint at the thought of treating a woman's particular health concerns, you would know that no precaution is fully effective. None. If you had asked me months ago, I would have happily confirmed that for you."

The doctor stumbled backward, bracing himself on the back of the pew immediately to his left. He looked ashen, drained of all his arrogant assumption. "I called her a liar," he choked, "and a ... a fair few other things. I was hurt, you understand. Lashing out."

"I'm afraid I understand all too well," Heloise whispered, her voice seething with restraint. Oh, how she wished to be a man in that moment, so that she might deliver a sound blow directly to Richard's cheek. "She went through everything alone, and you would have been happy to let her continue to do so."

"Imagine," Rose pondered, wrapping an arm around Heloise's waist to keep her from stepping forward, "the guilt you must feel. It is unconscionable. How fortunate that you have been granted an opportunity to make it right."

"I have?" Garber said thinly, staring past both women and out the window, presumably haunted by his own behavior.

"I will draw up the license application along with the lad's birth certificate," the reverend announced with an air of assumed joviality. "And allow me to be the first to congratulate you, Dr. Garber. You are luckier than most."

Heloise raised her eyes to meet the reverend's and found them narrowed upon the doctor's back. He looked as though he had a great deal to say on the matter as well, out of earshot of mixed company.

"Thank you, Reverend," Rose replied sweetly. "I will see Lady Heloise home."

All three of them turned their backs on Dr. Garber, moving toward a brighter day ahead. Heloise thought she did not imagine that the rest of the town turned their backs on him too.

20

Rose had insisted she eat a cup of porridge on the ride back to the dower house. She would hear no argument and watched intently until every last morsel had been consumed.

"I will see to Abigail, bring her food, and have Boudicea returned to our stables," she told Heloise while her mouth was too full to argue. "I will also be the one to explain to Gideon what happened in the church this morning. I fear it will take some gentle framing of the situation to avoid unsettling him."

Heloise narrowed her eyes at that, but did not comment. Gideon hated anything that set voices to whispering, and she had certainly done exactly that this morning. She was not sorry.

Richard might not make a loving husband to Abigail, but he'd make a respectable one with a reasonable fortune. It would be a better life than raising the boy alone, especially with an aging mother. Perhaps, in time, affection might once again sprout between them.

"Get some sleep," Rose instructed as the carriage ground to a halt outside of the dower house. As Heloise moved to exit the carriage, Rose reached out to touch her wrist and said gently, "You have earned your rest."

Heloise nodded silently and made her way into the house. It was still dark and quiet inside, with only a couple of parlor maids flitting past to see to their early duties.

She looked into the drawing room, but it no longer had anyone in it, which she supposed was fair enough, considering she had been gone for at least half a day. She climbed the stairs, the muscles in her legs aching with each step, and stopped first in the nursery to look in on her daughter.

Callie slept as angelically as she ever had, her blankets tossed back and her little limbs sprawled every which way on her little bed. Heloise felt a keen ache in her heart that she could not quite put a name to. What had changed since the last time she had spoken with her child?

She turned over her shoulder to stop one of the maids in her path. "Is the lieutenant still here?" she asked, remembering the last thing he'd said to her.

I'll be waiting.

The maid blushed and nodded. "Yes, My Lady. Your mother insisted he sleep in the blue room, but he's only just retired. The two of them stayed up all through the night and past the sunrise awaiting your return."

"And my mother?"

Chapter 20

"Asleep as well, My Lady," the girl replied. "She told us to only wake her if the house was falling down about us."

Heloise nodded, pulling the door of the nursery shut and sending the maid on her way. She did not speculate on what her mother and Callum had talked about for hours on end, with nothing to occupy them but anticipation of her presence. She did take some solace, at least, that she would not have an audience for the conversation that must happen with him now.

She crossed the house, past her own bedroom, and stopped outside of the door to the blue room, an outfitted bedroom that was intended for Callie when she was old enough to leave the nursery. She took a bracing breath and turned the doorknob, slipping inside with complete disregard for the shocked faces of any household staff who observed her doing so.

She locked the door behind her.

Callum was asleep, his back to her, rising and falling in the peaceful rhythm of oblivion. She kept her eyes on him, peeling off her layers of clothing until nothing remained but her shift. She climbed into bed behind him, carefully lifting the coverlet to slip beneath. She noted, pausing for a beat with breathless surprise, that he was cradling Callie's rag doll against his chest.

She pulled the blankets up to her shoulders as she slid into the bed. She melded herself to the back of him, pressing her cheek into the space between his shoulder blades, and inhaled deeply the scent of him.

If this would be the end of his love for her, she would at least make a final memory or two. She thought about whispering to him, attempting to wake him. She racked her mind for how she might start her speech. She found the words floating into her thoughts drifted away as soon as she reached out to grasp them, dancing on the haze of exhaustion that crept over her body.

It was in this way that she fell asleep with Callum Laughlin wrapped in her embrace.

---

*C*allum awoke with the strangest sensation of contentment, as though he had carried the magic of the dreamworld with him back into reality. It took him a moment, blinking the sleep from his eyes, returning to the limitations of his own body, but he did feel her before he saw her.

Her arm was looped under his arm and clasped upon the front of his shoulder, her head buried into his back with the warmth of her breath tickling at his spine. He did not want to move lest he shatter this moment or realize that it was, somehow, still only a dream.

Once he was certain that, somehow, this was real, he took her hand and eased it onto his chest so that he might roll onto his back. He coiled his arm around her and pulled her into the crook of his shoulder, lowering his lips to her brow and inhaling the sweet, earthy scent of her hair, which was loose and wild around them both.

He didn't know how long he'd slept. It must have been hours. The darkness that had settled over him in sleep had carried him through Heloise Somers crawling into bed next to him, without even a hint of waking. For the first time, he had been able to truly sleep in her arms, with no lingering concern about being discovered puncturing his path to oblivion.

He had not expected staying awake through the night to be so difficult. After all, he had done longer stretches of sleeplessness over the years as a means of survival. He thought, somehow, that discovering little Caroline, speaking with her, had spent his energy more than any grueling march across rough terrain ever had. By the time the sun had begun to glimmer through the windows of the drawing room, he was struggling to keep his head up.

The dowager had silenced any objections and shuffled him up to a guest bedroom to sleep through his prolonged wait for Heloise's return. He hoped that it was her way of giving her blessing, when she easily could have turned him out or attempted to convince him that his assumptions were wrong.

"Go back to sleep," Heloise murmured, turning her face into his shirt so that her hair fell across her eyes. "Not enough sleep."

He chuckled, despite all the dire things that loomed between them, stroking her hair between his fingers. "Rest as long as you need," he whispered. "Your night was likely more trying than mine."

"Likely," she repeated, peeking up at him through her tresses of hair. "Abigail is well."

"And the child?"

"A baby boy. William. He is whole, healthy, and soon to be legitimized."

Callum raised his eyebrows in genuine surprise. He had not heard the first whisper of speculation as to the father of Abigail's child.

"It was Dr. Garber," Heloise said impatiently. "I confronted him in the church and shamed him before the township. Gideon will be furious, of course, but the dear doctor will have no choice now but to do the honorable thing."

"He might flee," Callum said without thinking. He winced as soon as the words had left his mouth. That was what he had done, was it not?

"No," Heloise said, stretching out next to him and brushing the hair from her face. "Not if he wishes to continue to practice as a physician with any degree of success or be received in London. Now that I've made a scene, my brother will enforce propriety. He can be counted on for that."

"Yes, he can," Callum agreed.

She was quiet for a moment, staring at her hand over his heart. It was as though if neither of them mentioned the child they'd made for just a moment longer, things could be as they were.

"Heloise," he began, but she spoke over him in an urgent whisper.

"I will not tell Gideon—or anyone—should you wish to leave us," she finally said. "My mother would likewise keep our secret. You need never claim her, if it is not what you wish."

He thought, for a moment, that he was frozen in place, struck so blindly by her words that he'd turned to stone. She didn't move either, nor did she raise her eyes to look at him, instead keeping her gaze fixed on her hand, which rose and fell with his breath.

"I have always loved you," he finally said, reaching up to cup her hand with his own. "Since we were children, I have loved you. I have never wanted another woman the way I want you, and I never will. The only time I have felt anything even close was yesterday, when I saw her face and knew she was ours."

She did turn her face up at that, her eyes searching his own as he spoke.

"I should not have decided on my own what was best for our future," he whispered. "I convinced myself, somehow, that you could read my thoughts and that you would know I had gone to make my mark and build our fortune. I believed that you would be here, suspended in time, until I was able to return. You were right that day in the barn, that I was too proud to start our lives with your dowry money. I did not think I could find myself entirely worthy of you until I could match what Society expects for a lady's hand. I couldn't abide the thought that I would be seen by others as unworthy of you, or worse, that you would be looked down upon for having me."

"You have always been such a snob," she said, the ghost of a smile on her lips. "Worse than Gideon, even."

"A snob?" he echoed, genuinely surprised. "I was a stable boy!"

"Mm, with far more rigid beliefs about the rules of Society than many a member of the *ton*," she replied. "I hear you got your mother quite up in arms with assumptions about her misery in service shortly after arriving."

He frowned. He hadn't apologized for that, still. The fire had overshadowed everything else, cauterizing the wound in their relationship out of sheer necessity. Besides, part of him still felt justified in wishing to rescue her from a life of toil and subservience. It did not feel wrong to him. Was he truly a snob? Was she truly content with her lot in life, proud of it, even?

Heloise continued, unconcerned with the crisis in identity she'd just awoken within him. "In any event, you were not wrong to fear censure and ridicule. We would have been pelted with plenty of both, if Gideon hadn't put a stop to it entirely. He has changed much since the last time you saw him."

"Changed enough that he will not balk when you reveal who the father of your child truly is?"

She bit her lip, hesitating long enough in answering that he knew it was still a real possibility.

He groaned, dropping a hard kiss onto the top of her head. "So it seems our trials are not yet at an end," he said. "If you will have me, I would like for the three of us to be a true family."

"You, me, and that other woman you're cradling?"

He glanced over at his other arm, his confusion dissolving into amusement at the sight of Caroline's well-worn rag doll still nestled in the crook of his arm. "I will have to insist that she joins us," he said somberly. "I've grown rather attached."

Heloise giggled, swiping at the doll and tossing it on the bedside table. "I will not be displaced for your mistresses, Callum Laughlin."

"Oh, making rules already, are we?" he teased. "What else?"

"Hm. I do not want to leave Yorkshire," she replied, her hand beginning to trace circles over his chest. "I should never feel at home anywhere far from here, and I do not wish to take Callie away from so much family."

"Done," he agreed. "I still wish to pursue a business in horses, which would mean we could not live directly in the township."

"Yes, a country house is my preference as well," she mused, "though I still would continue my services as they are required. I love my work."

"I would insist that our child takes my surname when you do, of course."

"And that she no longer calls me Auntie Hel?" Heloise replied dreamily. "It would usually be a complication that we were not wed at the time of her birth, but the reverend said something today that makes me think we might be able to accomplish what we wish, should he be sympathetic to our cause."

He smiled to hear her talk so. "So does that mean you will marry me, Heloise Somers?"

"I will," she decided, reaching up to cup his cheek as she raised her lips to his. "Pending further negotiations, of course."

He raised his brows, curious and perhaps a little concerned as to what this could mean, but as the heat of her kisses pulled him into their spell, and their bodies tangled beneath the sheets of this borrowed bed, he found he was willing to negotiate further after all.

21

In the aftermath of their morning together, they had decided upon two things: first, that Callie should be told the truth first, before anyone else, and second that revealing the news within a family group, all at once, would prevent any overly dramatic reactions.

"You mean one of your brothers attempting to strangle me, I presume?" Callum had asked, hair falling over his eyes as he pulled his boots on.

"Yes. Though I imagine your mother will be none too pleased with me either," Heloise responded, weaving a braid into her hair from her perch on the big blue bed. "At the very least, she's never seemed the type to resort to direct violence."

Callum scoffed. "Says you."

When they emerged from the room, the staff that observed it kept their eyes averted and heads down, though doubtless whispers were already brewing belowstairs. Callum went immediately to the dining room in the hopes of intercepting

Chapter 21

Ruthie Somers at luncheon, while Heloise went to her own chambers to change into a clean dress.

She chose a loose gown of daisy yellow with her daughter in mind and tucked the little rag doll into the deep pocket fashioned into the skirts. Today was to be a very important day. She believed she was prepared for it, after the mental turmoil of the last few weeks had forged her into a keen sort of steel, but all the same, when she entered the dining room to find her mother and her fiancé in low conversation, her heart seemed to lodge itself right in the center of her throat.

Ruthie's eyes caught sight of her first, and far from the frown of disapproval Heloise had anticipated, her mother's face cracked into a joyous grin, eye wrinkles and all. "Good morning," she sang. "I am so pleased, my beautiful girl."

"With?" Heloise replied, still erring toward caution as she swept into the room to be seated at the foot of the table.

"Why, your impending nuptials, of course!" Ruthie beamed. "For so much, truly. I trust Miss Collins is well?"

"She is," Heloise confirmed, raising her eyebrows at Callum. "I thought we were going to announce to everyone at once?"

"We will," he told her. "But your mother has agreed to ensure everyone is gathered at the appropriate time so that we may do so. She already knew, after all."

"Only just," Ruthie added. "Caroline and Reggie are at the manor house today, so perhaps we should all make our way across the green now. If anyone is currently out or attending the township, it will give us time to call them back to the house."

Heloise nodded, another lurch of anxiety firing off in her

stomach. This was it, then. The end of her secrets had arrived. A brand new life was over the horizon, somehow, when just yesterday it had seemed so far from her grasp.

She forced herself to eat, just some toast and a few slices of dried pear, and did not argue when Ruthie suggested they take a carriage over. She met Callum's eye several times, wondering if he was experiencing a turmoil on par with her own, but every time, those black eyes twinkled back at her with such unbridled happiness that she felt silly for having any worries at all.

In the carriage, he held her hand. That little gesture stirred all manner of emotions within her, particularly that it was happening within her mother's view. With Callum, every affection had come to feel forbidden, every touch by necessity clandestine. Allowing him this intimacy, so brazenly displayed, was both a luxurious indulgence and so alien as to fill her with unnecessary worry, as though somehow being too happy or too optimistic might horribly backfire.

She clung to his hand as though it were the only thing that kept this reality fixed in place.

He had asked her that morning to tell him of their daughter, even though he had met her himself and spent an entire night and morning asking every question he could think of from her grandmother. She had recounted the stories that first came to mind, of the way she seemed to always soothe Reggie in a way no one else could, of her fondness for food that made crumbs and sticky sweets, of the way Nero watched her but never got too close, as though she were his charge and he a consummate professional who did not cross the bounds of propriety with that which he must protect.

Chapter 21

"There is something I've been wondering," he had said, nuzzling into the crown of her head as she'd clung to him in drowsy bliss. "The girl Alex married, the icy blonde. Could she be the girl you once told me of, from school? The one you hated?"

"She is," Heloise had confirmed. "I no longer hate her. Though to be honest, she is very little changed."

He had laughed, of course, at the way fate had toyed with them all.

When they reached the house, Ruthie had made ready to dispatch herself immediately in search of all required members of their family's meeting.

"Mama," Hel had said, catching her wrist before she could speed away. "Please invite the reverend too. He will be family soon enough, I think."

"Hm," Ruthie had replied, the pleasure apparent in her face. "We shall see."

The Somerton nursery was on the third floor of the house, in a large space overlooking a frozen pond and snow bank. It had once been a room for entertaining, with billiards and card tables rather than cribs and plush toys, but Heloise rather thought it had found its true calling under Rose's modifications.

The children were at play when they arrived, and rather than interrupt their fun, Heloise nodded toward a set of chairs so that they might simply sit together and enjoy watching their daughter at her happiest. Reggie, by contrast, also reminded them of how singularly lucky they had been, to create offspring that was so naturally well-behaved.

Callie caught sight of them over her tower of blocks and waved in the pure, unbridled expression of pleasure that could only be shown by children. She stood and made her way over to where they sat without beckoning nor encouragement, as though she knew something important awaited her other than stacking blocks today. The nursemaids did not follow, both presently occupied with preventing Master Reggie from vaulting himself directly through the window facing the grounds.

"Hi Callie," Callum said, easing out of the chair to kneel before her, rag doll in hand. "Thank you for lending me your doll. She kept all of the bad dreams away."

"She is good," Callie agreed, taking her back and holding her in a tight hug. "All better?" she asked him hopefully.

"All better," he confirmed with a smile.

"Callie," Heloise said softly, kneeling next to Callum and putting a hand out to hold the child's. "Do you know what a mama and a papa are?"

Callie bit her lip. "Yes," she said after a moment, "but I haven't any."

"You do," Heloise corrected, her voice gentle against the little crack in her heart. "Of course you do, darling. This is your papa. You see? His eyes are the same as yours."

She turned those big, dark eyes up to Callum's, blinking and curious. "You are my papa?"

"Yes." He nodded, his own voice sounding near to breaking. "I have been waiting a very long time to meet you."

She frowned, considering this. "And my mama?"

Chapter 21

Hel and Callum exchanged a glance. He spoke first.

"Auntie Heloise is your mama."

"No." Callie shook her head, her auburn ringlets swaying over her cheeks. "She is my auntie."

"Callie," Hel murmured, touching her daughter's hair. "I am your mama, but we had to keep it a secret until your papa came back. Would you like it if you called me Mama from now on, instead of Auntie?"

"Mama," Callie repeated, testing the sound of the word on her tongue. She turned to Callum, extending her other hand for his. "Papa."

Heloise laughed, though it sounded for all the world like a sob.

"Yes," Callie decided. "Mama and Papa."

"We are going to be a family now," Heloise told her, squeezing her little hand. "We will have our own house with lots of horses to ride, little one. And maybe one day some brothers and sisters for you."

Callie simply smiled back at her parents.

Even if she was too small to understand the full weight of what was being said, she seemed to grasp that these things made everyone very happy, and so she was happy too. "Can I go play?" she asked.

"Of course, yes," Heloise replied, leaning forward to drop a cheek on Callie's head. "Have fun."

She smiled broadly, perching forward to kiss each of her parents on their cheeks. When she skipped away, back to her play with her cousin, Hel and Callum sat back and watched, both smiling through the tears on their cheeks.

House Somers was no stranger to secret family meetings, each of them centered around topics that the scandal sheets would have delighted to overhear. Perhaps that was why Gideon Somers looked so dour, before anything had been said at all.

They gathered at Ruthie's behest, sprinkled throughout the sitting room. Heloise suspected that they were anticipating a wedding announcement from their mother, and as such had not reacted with surprise when Reverend Halliwell arrived and took a seat next to the fire, striking up friendly conversation with Rose.

Sheldon Bywater had not been expressly invited, but was there anyhow, his pregnant dog snoozing with her head in his lap.

The Blakelys had returned from Leeds a few hours prior, so mercifully they were taking some rest and would not notice a conspicuous congregation of the family members. Gloriana sat placidly next to Alex. If she knew what was coming, her face did not show it.

The last to arrive were Callum himself and Mrs. Laughlin. This, of course, did raise some eyebrows, though Gideon's lowered and drew together, his disconcert apparent for all to see. Not for the first time, Heloise felt her heart give a queasy leap in anticipation of what she must say, finally, to everyone.

Mrs. Laughlin looked fairly green herself. Either Callum had told her some of the news prior to bringing her into the sitting room or she was concerned that this meeting was to dismiss her. Hel hoped it was the former.

Ruthie closed the door, shooing away hovering staff and turning a bright, unconcerned smile to the room. "That's everyone then!" she announced. "Shall we begin?"

Heloise took a steadying breath and pushed herself to her feet, drawing the eyes of the gathered family to her. She hoped she did not sway where she stood. The thick wool of her yellow dress anchored her a little with its weight.

"Everyone here, aside from Reverend Halliwell, knows that Caroline is my daughter," she began.

Rose immediately startled, her eyes cutting to Gloriana, who returned her gaze and gave a little shrug.

"Heloise!" Gideon gasped, only ceasing in whatever lecture he was about to deliver by the expression on her face as she turned to him.

The reverend did not move at all, his face still pleasantly blank as he listened to Heloise speak.

"Please, Gideon," she said. "I must say everything now or lose my gall completely. Caroline is my daughter. You know it to be true. She is my child and her father is here with us today."

Callum appeared at her shoulder, placing a steadying hand there. Her eyes flickered shut, battling off a wave of anxiety that rose in her. She did not like the way Alex had immediately straightened in his chair, nor the sudden furious cut of Gideon's eyes from herself to Callum. She could not drown out the shocked gasp that had emitted from Mrs. Laughlin, whose hands now covered her mouth.

"We planned to marry in secret," she said, "years ago. We knew that people would not approve, and so Callum took the opportunity to head to the Continent in search of valor and fortune, in the hopes that he would return of a status suitable for courting me."

"I did not know she was with child," he added, his back straight and his jaw set. "I would never have left if I had known."

Sheldon Bywater grumbled something unintelligible at that, glaring at the couple through narrowed eyes.

"We intend to marry now," Heloise continued, wishing to have this done as quickly as possible. "We are not here to ask permission nor to debate the matter. We will be married. The only obstacle to our future will come in the matter of Caroline's legitimacy, which does not currently exist."

"Ah," the reverend said with a nod, suddenly understanding his part in this. He turned to Ruthie with a tilt of his head. "I imagine that the child has no birth records whatsoever, then? If she was not born in the Americas, as I believed."

"She does not," Rose confirmed in a businesslike tone. "Only the notes we kept internally here at Somerton to record her time and date of birth and weight and so on."

"Well, then it seems to me that such documents must be drawn up immediately," the reverend mused, scratching his chin. "If Lady Heloise and the lieutenant had, say, eloped to Scotland prior to his military service in secret, the child's legitimacy would be valid."

Heloise released a shaky breath, uncertain if she should allow relief to crash over her just yet. "Yes, though we would need to say true vows as well, lest the marriage be a lie."

"Naturally!" the reverend agreed, as though he were affronted by the suggestion that he had meant anything else. "We will record it as a renewal of vows, after the original records were destroyed in the fire."

"I suppose neither of you are interested in our blessing before trotting off down the aisle?" Alex said.

"Callum would probably appreciate it," Heloise told him, "but it is not necessary."

"Humph," mumbled Alex.

"It will be quite a scandal," Rose put in with a frown and a glance at her husband, "but a romantic one, at the very least. A secret marriage is preferable to a child born out of wedlock, after all."

Gideon was silent, but his color was high. Heloise imagined he was containing an explosion within his stony visage.

Mrs. Laughlin was still covering her mouth, apparently frozen in shock at these revelations, one right after the other.

Heloise met her eye, guilt keen in her chest at this deception in particular. "I am so sorry," she said. "I wanted to tell you many times, but was not brave enough to do so."

"Oh, child," Mrs. Laughlin cried, dropping her hands away and marching across the room to fold Heloise into her embrace.

Hel was not certain she'd ever been hugged like this by anyone, nor how to respond to it. She tentatively returned the embrace, patting the other woman on the back and attempting not to appear too relieved when the hug was broken so that Mrs. Laughlin could gaze into her face. "I have a granddaughter!" she breathed, squeezing her eyes shut and shaking her head.

To Callum, she said, "I ought to box your ears!"

He nodded, giving her a weak smile as she wrapped him into one of her hugs as well, which seemed a fair sight nicer than ear boxing to Heloise. She patted them both on the arms as she drew back, her face shiny with emotion.

Gideon sighed loudly, casting his eyes heavenward. "So, then, what are our next steps? Laughlin, do you have a plan for housing your wife and child or was all that military service for naught?"

"I've a mind to buy a property on the outskirts of the township," Callum replied, "and breed horses."

"We will not go far," Heloise assured her brother, setting a hand on Callum's arm to emphasize that her decision was made. "Somerton is still our home. If you are grousing over the dispersal of my dowry, I will simply need to begin charging for my midwifery services."

"Oh, darling, Gideon doesn't control your dowry," Ruthie said with a wave of her hand. "I do."

Rose cleared her throat, interrupting whatever sniping was sure to follow a statement like that. "Reverend Halliwell, how do you suggest we go about this? Should we send the pair up to Scotland tonight to cement new vows or apply for a proper license through the traditional channels?"

"I favor Scotland," Ruthie put in. "George and I can accompany the couple as witnesses and have our own vows done at the same time."

A ring of silence followed this declaration, broken only by another beleaguered sigh from Gideon, and his wife saying over it, "Oh, Ruthie, congratulations!" and Alex demanding, "So whose house will you be living in?!"

It was a relief, the explosion of chaos and noise and the pelting of questions, even those directed at Heloise herself. Somehow, the worst part was over.

Gideon looked uncomfortable, but not enraged. He watched her with a silent contemplation that she knew would result in quite a talking-to later, in private. Alex seemed to be overtly enjoying the upheaval, grinning and leaning back to watch the hubbub unfold. Ruthie had crossed the room to kiss her fiancé smack on the mouth in front of everyone while Sheldon Bywater watched in affectionate awe.

Rose and Gloriana both rose from their seats, approaching Heloise with talk of bridal planning, even for a haphazard elopement, though their voices were difficult to discern over all the shouting.

Heloise thought it was rather beautiful, truth be told.

House Somers had always thrived in the midst of chaos.

22

It was, all things considered, the strangest elopement ever to grace the scandal sheets. Or at least that was what Callum was told for years to come.

"I wish to control the narrative before it can be distorted," Gideon Somers had said at the first inn on the way to Moorvale. "It is the only way to avoid surprises."

"Mm, so Mr. d'Aubrey is coming out of retirement?" the viscountess teased, giggling at the way her husband's color rose at the cryptic jibe.

Apparently, one did not often elope in tandem with one's mother, who also intended to elope, much less with the entire family in tow. Further, Callum was informed by a very confident Gloriana Somers that elopements generally happened right at the border between England and Scotland, usually in the city of Gretna Green. It would create interest and whispers that they were riding another entire day north, to be wed in a traditional fashion, in the rustic, far-flung Moorvale.

Chapter 22

It had taken a little less than a week to organize everything. After that tense meeting in the Somerton sitting room, Callum had thought they'd simply ride for the border that night, but the women of House Somers would hear nothing of it. He included his mother in that group. She was, he supposed, one of them now.

George Halliwell had been his most ardent supporter in the wake of the full revelation of his indiscretion, some four years prior. Gideon Somers had barely said a word directly to him, and Alex had only shaken his hand, given him a wry smile, and wished him good luck with his hellcat of a sister.

It was GIdeon that inspired the most guilt, and so, at that first inn, after the ladies retired for the evening, he resolved to make his amends in any way that he could. He ordered two pints of ale and made his way over to the table, shoved in the far corner of the inn, where the viscount was frowning over a piece of parchment as he wrote his scandal letter to the *Evening Standard*.

He did not appear to react when Callum slid into the seat across from him and placed one of the pints next to his candle and paper. Instead, he remained fixed on the sentence he was crafting until he could put a satisfied period at the end of it. Then he looked up, his brows raising in surprise.

"I thought you were Sheldon," he said. "No one else buys me drinks."

"Consider it the first of many," Callum had replied. "I wished to speak with you in private, Lord Somers."

"All right," Gideon replied, taking a sip of the ale and leaning back in his chair. "You have me."

"I have gone back and forth over what to say, My Lord. I wish to apologize for violating your trust and the opportunities you were willing to give me to advance my station, but at the same time, I have no regrets whatsoever regarding that summer with Heloise. As I said before, I only wish I had known she was with child. I love your sister, but I also feel ashamed of how I misused my position with you."

Gideon considered this, taking another sip of the ale and watching Callum with a steady gaze. He sighed and set his cup down with a little shake of his head.

"Lieutenant ... Callum," he started. "I have been similarly conflicted. My immediate reaction was to defend my sister's honor in the most primitive way possible, but my wife, ever the steady hand, reminded me of something important. The only reason I am married at all, much less to the woman I have always loved, is because of what happened to Heloise."

"I don't follow," Callum confessed, his heart hammering in his chest.

"I thought that if I wed immediately and spirited a bride up to Somerton, I might be able to pass the child off as our own. It was not a well thought-out plan," Gideon Somers said, and, to Callum's deep shock, *smiled*. "I was in such a panic that I attempted to call in a poorly made marriage contract negotiated by my father, to a bride who was not at all interested in the role. Rose stepped in and offered to marry me, not knowing what a mess was waiting for me back home, and if she had not, I cannot say how things might have gone. I scarcely remember what our family was like before she was part of it."

"I see," Callum replied, though of course, he did not truly.

Chapter 22

"I will tell you what I told Richard Garber," Gideon decided, draining the last of his pint. "If you are a bad husband, I will hear of it and you will lose your wife, but not your obligations as a husband. I daresay I have far more faith in your performance as a spouse than I do in his. Treat my sister as she deserves to be treated, love my niece as she deserves to be loved, and I will welcome you as a brother and a friend."

This thought had stuck with Callum for the remainder of the journey north, playing in his head even as they alighted from their carriages at the doors of Hawk Hill, Sheldon Bywater's historic estate.

"I rather envy you, Heloise," Gloriana had said to her once-nemesis as they walked into the massive reception hall. "I always imagined I'd get married in a castle."

"It was my castle, dear," Reverend Halliwell had responded with a chuckle. "Just as grand in God's eyes."

"You'll want to keep a close eye on the weans," Sheldon had said to the nursemaids. "Lots of places to run amok here, and that Reginald will do so if given the opportunity."

"We really should have left them at Somerton with my parents," Gloriana commented with a frown. "It's not a matter of *if* Reggie wanders into trouble, it's a matter of *when.*"

Reggie had beamed his half-toothed smile at his aunt, as though she had bestowed upon him the most gratuitous praise, but remained at his nanny's side, her hand firmly gripped in his own.

"Let us all rest," Rose Somers had suggested. "Tomorrow will be a busy day."

---

*H*eloise Somers had never put much thought into what she would wear when she wed. She had derided the girls who dreamed of wedding gowns and sugared cakes and titled, well-bred husbands as silly and beneath her. It wasn't until the morning of her own wedding that she realized how silly she'd been, and how much she wished she knew what to wear for her own wedding day.

Gloriana and Rose had parsed her wardrobe before they'd left Yorkshire, looking for something worthy of a wedding dress. They had ignored her objections and insistence that it did not matter, but seemed dissatisfied with her practical wardrobe, built for function rather than style.

"You shall wear one of mine," Gloriana had decided, spinning away from the wardrobe in exasperation. "We are of a size."

"Oh, shall I?" Heloise had responded, perhaps with more heat than she actually felt.

The dress Gloriana had chosen was a pale blue, embroidered with Queen Anne's lace at the hem and a pair of red-breasted robins in flight along the line of the skirt. Heloise had never seen her wear it, and apparently never would, for Gloriana made it clear that the dress was a gift on the morning of the wedding, when she arrived without invitation, flanked by two lady's maids, to prepare Heloise for her marriage.

Chapter 22

"I wish to wear my hair down," Heloise had said, but otherwise made no demands.

"Something old, something new," Gloriana had mused, "the dress is new, but not borrowed, as it is a gift. The necklace is old, is it not?"

"It was my grandmother's," Heloise affirmed, brushing the pearls at her throat. "The dress has blue in it."

"Yes." The other woman nodded. "Rose suggested you wear the earrings she wore for her own wedding, so those will count as borrowed. I will go and retrieve them, and a sixpence to tuck into your shoes."

She had gone before Heloise had occasion to argue, so she simply sat in place and allowed the two maids to fuss over her, combing her long red hair and coaxing the curls into uniform ringlets with the assist of a heated wand. They dabbed rose oil on her lips and eyelids, and braided the sides of her hair into an ornate crown from which the rest of her waist-length hair spilled elegantly down her back.

When Gloriana returned with the earrings and the coin, she gasped in earnest at the presentation of Heloise in her bridal finery. Her ice-blue eyes seemed to melt a little, tears escaping down her porcelain cheeks as she came forward to secure Rose's earrings onto Heloise's ears.

"Why are you crying?" Heloise had asked with friendly amusement.

"Because you are beautiful," Gloriana had responded, averting her eyes and turning her back. "And because I made you feel ugly, once. I didn't see you as I see you now, and I am so sorry."

"Glory, it is all in the past," Heloise had responded, pushing herself to her feet and walking around to face Gloriana. "Remember what I said. I was awful to you too. I was jealous and childish and I would take it back if I could. You are my sister. Now and forever. And sisters always clash when they are young."

Gloriana had burst into tears, wrapping her arms around Heloise and pulling her tight against her body.

Heloise, to her genuine surprise, found herself tearing up as well, and returning the embrace with a ferocity she did not know she possessed.

"Oh, no, no," Gloriana had tutted. "Red eyes will not do."

But both had cried all the same.

The Moorvale parish vicar awaited them in the dining hall, a massive medieval behemoth of a room, which had been arranged into tables for the wedding breakfast on one side, and a makeshift chapel on the other.

Ruthie and George married first, with Heloise watching from the doorway. Gideon gave their mother away, and though she was too far to hear the vows spoken, Heloise felt confident that her mother spoke them with feeling. When she kissed the good reverend, she seemed an entirely different woman than the starched matriarch she had always been. Instead, she was the lady who had served porridge to the villagers, clad in simple white and framed by the beauty of stained glass.

Her breath caught when Callum approached the makeshift pulpit, the Moorvale vicar stepping aside for Reverend Halliwell to oversee the second wedding.

Chapter 22

George knelt and whispered to Callie, who turned and ran to Heloise's position, her little yellow gown fluttering around her tiny legs.

It would add to the scandal, she knew, to have her own daughter accompany her down the aisle, rather than a father or brother or guardian. She was satisfied with the stir it would cause. It was worth it.

"It's time, Aun... I mean, Mama," Callie whispered, holding out her hand.

The two walked from the doors to the pulpit, and Heloise thought perhaps that she did feel beautiful in that moment, especially with the way the room seemed to hold its breath as it beheld her. Callum was grinning like a fool, watching the two of them approach, and when they reached him, he greeted his daughter first, sweeping her up into his arms and kissing her cheek before sending her giggling over to the pew to sit with her aunts and uncles.

Heloise noted with satisfaction that Sheldon Bywater was dabbing at his eyes. It would not have done for him to cry at Alex's wedding and not her own, after all. He was flanked on either side by supportive women: Echo on one side and Brenda Laughlin on the other. The older lady was patting him on his broad shoulders as she wiped at her own tears with a handkerchief.

"Dearly beloved," Reverend Halliwell began, raising his white eyebrows and smiling at them both. "We are gathered together here in the sight of God, and in the face of this congregation, to join together this man and this woman in holy matrimony."

It seemed to Heloise that she had heard these vows many

times in her life, but never truly listened to them until she was saying them herself. She wondered if every bride felt a surreal sense of the world on her wedding day, or if perhaps she had so firmly believed she would never marry that it was taking time for her mind to catch up with her body.

Later, she would only remember saying "I do," and the kiss that followed, soft and chaste and unbearably sweet. She would remember those dark eyes, lit with so much joy that they sparkled, and the way her daughter ran into her arms as the applause exploded from their tiny audience.

From that day to her last, she would remember the moment she became Heloise Laughlin.

EPILOGUE

FIVE YEARS LATER

*C*allie Laughlin loved the full moon.

On a night like this one, when it was fat and bright and only just risen, it sent a wash of ethereal light over the moors, turning the earth into something from a fairy story, something magical and romantic.

Her parents always said you could find your true love more easily under the full moon. She wondered if she had a true love, and if so, if he loved the full moon as well. Her mother always said to be patient about love, for it can take some time. Her father always said to be exacting, and never settle for anything other than the perfect mate.

She clung to the window of the carriage as the night-lit scenery rolled past, wide-eyed and enchanted by every silver blade of grass. She was keenly aware that she was awake later than she was supposed to be because Mama had gotten waylaid in the township with her work. It was almost a disappointment when the carriage reached their house, the horses slowing as they approached the drive.

"May I tuck Brendan in?" she asked without turning to look at her mother.

"If he is still awake, perhaps," Heloise Laughlin answered, reaching out to stroke her daughter's hair. "What story will you tell him?"

"The Princess and the Stable Boy, of course," Callie answered, tossing her mother a derisive roll of the eyes over her shoulder. "You know that it is his favorite."

"Is it his favorite or yours?" Heloise teased, chuckling at her daughter's scoff of indignation.

Callie ran ahead of her mother, eager to get into the house and to her brother's bedroom before the little bug could drift off to sleep. She had promised him, after all, that she would tell him stories tonight.

"What's the hurry?" her father exclaimed as she flew past him on her way to the staircase. "No greeting for me?"

"Papa," she groaned, turning and giving him a quick, tight squeeze around the middle. "I have to hurry to Brendan, before he goes to sleep."

"You might already be too late." Callum Laughlin laughed, releasing his child so that she could continue her mission. "He was drowsing over dinner more than an hour ago."

Callie did not say so, but she would wake him if he had already drifted off. He wouldn't mind.

She heard her mother and father greeting one another behind her and the smack of a greeting kiss. There was low murmuring about boring adult matters and their upcoming trip to London to see Uncle Alex and Aunt Glory. Brendan did not want them to go, but Callie was looking forward to staying at Somerton for a few weeks, being close to her grandparents and cousins.

It would be great fun.

She pushed open the door to the nursery and smiled in relief at her three-year-old brother sitting upright, waiting for her. He had their big, brown mutt, Cleo, at the foot of his bed.

Cleo had no interest in stories over the embrace of sleep and did not even lift her head in acknowledgement, choosing instead to keep snoring.

Callie gave her a scratch between the ears anyway, dropping a kiss on her head before looking up at her brother.

"I heard you," he said by way of explanation, yawning behind his hand. "Story?"

"Yes, of course," she whispered, planting another kiss on his mussed hair and sitting on the side of the bed. At eight, she felt impossibly mature next to her little brother, and loved playing the part. "Where did we leave off?"

He yawned once more, blinking up at her with his green Somers eyes. "The knight was going to come home," he said, "and the princess was living in the village with the little princess."

"Ah, yes," she nodded, urging him to lie down and pulling the blanket up to his chin. "The knight arrived during a blizzard, and had to fight his way north to find his princess. Once he reached her, there was a great fire in the kingdom, forcing them to rescue the townsfolk before they could be together again. The princess was very mad at the knight for leaving, but she loved him still, and could not resist when he began to woo her again."

"What's woo?" Brendan asked.

"Being nice and sweet," Callie answered, though she was not entirely certain.

"Did she forgive him?" he asked, his forehead wrinkled up with concern.

"Well, he brought her flowers and wrote her poems until she trusted him again. Then she let him meet the little princess, and they got married, and lived happily ever after, but I'm not there yet. I'm only to the fire."

"Okay," her little brother sighed in relief. "The fire ..."

Callie nodded, closing her eyes and dredging up the image in her mind. "It was a grand adventure," she whispered. "I will tell you all about it."

AUTHOR'S NOTE

Thank you so much for reading! As an up-and-coming indie romance author, reviews can make or break my future as a writer. If you have a moment, please consider leaving me a review on Amazon, Bookbub, or Goodreads. It would mean the absolute world to me!

The Somerton Scandals has been an incredible journey. While this trilogy is complete, I promise that the Somers clan will pop up from time to time in later books. If you read *The Scoundrel and the Socialite*, you are already primed for my next trilogy, which will focus on Eleanor Applegate and Nathaniel Atlas and is coming to Amazon in Spring 2020.

Stay tuned for updates!

I also love to hear from my readers! If you have feedback, questions, or ever just want to say hi, you can reach me at Ava@AvaDevlin.com

FREE EBOOK!

Discover the Scandal that Started Them All ...

Lady Heloise Somers has always been wild, despite the best efforts of a dozen governesses, a posh finishing school, and her exasperated brother.

Callum Laughlin is the son of a housekeeper, whose dreams have always been of greatness—riches, glory, and, most of all, a red-haired hellion born far above his station. He would give anything to have Lady Heloise at his side and in his bed.

As the summer sun blazes over Yorkshire, Callum and Heloise can't resist the heat that draws them together, no matter how forbidden their passion may be. Secret trysts, rumbling storms, and dreams of something more weave together this sweet and steamy prequel to The Somerton Scandals, sparking the romance that changed House Somers forever.

Free eBook!

Click Here to Get Your Copy Today!

(Or head to AvaDevlin.com to claim your exclusive copy)

Printed in Great Britain
by Amazon